Cover design by Nick Skerten

Names, characters, places and incidents are either the product of the author's imagination or are used fictitiously, and any resemblance to any persons, living or dead, business establishments, events or locales is entirely coincidental.

ISBN: 9798391225201

SIX WEEK PSYCHOSIS

by

BRENDAN WYER

Listen. Listen listen listen. Got a little bit of time.

Help. Look at the heights I've sunk to. I joined the world of showbiz to spend days being shouted at by poshos in a freezing town and watching bad lines of script being repeated on an inhospitable bit of beach whilst I wondered how long I'd needed the loo. No really, I did. Can't you tell? It's the peak of my ambition.

Wait. Let me hold the wall. Ok. Look. I'm getting warm now that I've been indoors for the first time since five in the morning and I can move my hands, so let's get to it. I need to tell you, whilst I'm allowing any time left.

I got screamed at twice today. Yes, really. Only twice. It's nice to be noticed, isn't it? Something about the set-up, the marker was half a foot out of line, cost us ten minutes to re-set when the light was precarious. I didn't say anything, just got to work and moved it. I would have said something, a few weeks or months or years ago. Ah, I remember the woman I was then, back when I could laugh at life. What a pup. But no, I didn't say anything. Didn't get any thanks when I did move it, of course. Heard the Director Of Photography a few hours afterward saying that he'd be surprised if the scene was used in the final cut of the film. It had been written the night before after the director had demanded a solo scene with our lead actress, Zephiah. Or actor, I should say. Actor, actress, fuck, whatever. The scene was just her smoking in a sou'wester and DMs, and apparently looking erotic. Looked like a right nang to my eye, but then I'm not a director, or a man, or in lust with her.

Anyhow, the scene had to happen because they'd already taken some publicity shots with her dressed like that and they wanted her doing that and Hero, as the producer, wanted her doing that in the film because he thought it would look daft if we had her doing that in publicity but not in a scene. Oh, if only someone had the guts to tell him that they both look shit either way. Well, I suppose there's be an outside chance that someone could watch the final thing and stagger out of the cinema, furious that they didn't have a scene of the lead looking forlornly out into the English channel and smoking her head off. But that's predicated on a) this bloody shoot finishing and someone editing it into something approaching coherence, b) it being picked up for distribution, and c) anyone watching it. Four hours it took, all in all, and I can't even put my finger on what caused it to take so long, that's just the way it's gone over the last month or god knows when. When you have a hundred people who can't even agree on what county they're in or what an

Otter is, you have scant chance of anything going smoothly, even pointing a camera at an actress who doesn't have to do anything for half a minute.

Well, the static picture was daft in the first place, so having it in a moving image wouldn't make it any less so. You can't daft your way out of a corner. And I know I wasn't the only person on set thinking that. In fact, I'd be surprised if anyone apart from Hero and Zephiah thought it was worth losing time to. But they are the producer and the lead, so the rest of us had better keep our own council.

I have a good degree, you know. All the things I could have done. I hope I still can, if and when I escape. Have I broken myself doing this? I spent year after year to get into this kind of stuff. I've made films, my friend. So how did I end up running around here getting shouted at by a bunch of Henrys, Debs and Tarquins? I'm trying to remember, trying to pick apart the downward path I willingly lobbed myself down. I've spent most of my twenties doing it. Tell me will you, shadow, when you were this age was this the point where it hit you that time has gone and that it wouldn't be coming back? As in, most of the time of life when anyone on this earth can look at you and say – that's a youth. All right, all right, I know I'm young, but just look all the other little shits here, you can tell they're younger, can't you? They can, I may as well be a muttering crone for all they care. In the full flush of youth. Wish I could flush them downriver. Anyway, like I said. Only myself to blame.

Poshness, as well. That's the other undertow to the whole thing. Everyone is on this crew. Even the owl, even the dog. Seriously. Don't believe me? They don't talk about dinner, it's supper. I never heard anyone call it that until University, and even then it was one person everyone else took the piss out of. But no, here we go. A whole crew of people who may well have never been really hungry or cold in their cozy little lives. That's two they've got against me, super-youth and a sense of utter entitlement. Ease. I envy their sense of ease. It's like they've decided to do this on a whim. You know, like they realised they were nearing the end of their art history degree in St Andrews and had better have something to do afterward, so they picked up a phone and ended up working in film because it seemed like a fun thing to do. And they're having their fun, alright, it seems to me. Oh, they'll get tired, cold, wet, hungry (peckish more like). They'll feel that they're at the end of their tether, but that's just it, it's like elastic. It'll stretch so far, then at some point it'll ping back and they'll be pulled back in the warmth of god-knows-where, relaxing and not having to worry about whether they can pay the rent or whether they'll have to go back to a call centre job.

Ah, I'm losing time, I'm losing momentum to it all. I can feel films that I could create, put out there into the world, flying away from me, whirling away into the void and being dragged into the orbit of the open gob of a gargantuan, floating Hero, who swallows it, oblivious to it vanishing within.

Ugh. Sorry, I think it's the lack of sleep, these visions keep coming up and imprinting themselves on me, I can't help but share. Isn't that very filmmaker of me? I've got to get something down, but whenever I manage to find my notebook, just before I sleep, whatever I've tried to get down flies out of my brain, it's gone out into the waiting ocean and it'll never come back. Leaves me blank.

I was proud of myself, the other day. No, really. I got through a day of impossible tasks with no trip-ups, spillages or tears. As you may have gathered, that isn't usual in our little world, here. Carrying a cardboard tray of six teas in a high wind is enough to ask of someone if they've had a couple of hours sleep, and then had to make each to order (sugar, two sugars, milk, no milk, green tea, peppermint tea), but when they gave me another order of eight on top of that, I knew it'd be a test. Eight more people who will want their tea exactly now, exactly on time, and exactly as they ordered. Although they didn't tell you what they wanted, they've told someone who has told someone else who has now told you. And when you have to wind your way through a set's worth of cameras, honeywagons, cables, lights, more cameras, pre-fabs, tents and a flotilla of people who haven't ordered a tea off you yet, it's a task all right. I'd got eight made and punctured through one cardboard tray, held between my forearms straight, like a waiter proffering a main course, albeit with another cardboard tray of six on top, trying not to slop any of the lot as I made my way to the director, who was on the beach with the setting shot.

The secret is, with this kind of work, that you have to be secret. Even when you're balancing all that between your arms, trying not to scald yourself with any of the little liquid chicks, you don't want to break anyone else's concentration whilst trying to keep your own. Woe betide you if you do. The problem with this, I've found, is that some people in crews – always the same ones – find that all it takes for you to break their concentration if to simply exist in the same vicinity for a short amount of time. And that this usually correlates with them being in a frustrated mood. Make yourself as invisible as you can, elude everyone's attention as best possible, but if that ego is having a bad day your suppressed, tired exhalation as you enter the studio will be as catastrophically loud as a fart from Godzilla. And it will be answered with just as volcanic a reply.

Now another kind of person will allow you to pass in secrecy and do your job. But that's mostly because they don't know you day-to-day anyway, despite possibly having been cheeck-by-jowl with you for several weeks. Yep, they'll keep this level of ignoral going so far that even if you are trying to carry a café's worth of caffeine by your self, whilst not falling over, they still won't see you. Which means they'll walk into you. Which in turn means that you've probably been noticed by the first kind of person and you're being screamed at as soon as the coffee has hit the floor (seconds before you have).

No, I managed it today. A terrifying thought comes to me – am I getting good at this? Crap. No, can't, I'm just used to getting trapped. I've made films, I've directed - is this my metier? Is this actually where I'm supposed to be? Was my aim too high?

Anyway, I'd delivered the round of drinks, and was thinking that I wouldn't mind having a hot drink myself, when our Director gave me some direction.

'Lorna – thanks, would you mind getting Dermot from out of his tent and to the cue, here? We've left him ready ad no-one's seen him run out.'

Despite being noticed, I wasn't too keen on this. Not about him getting my name wrong. It's Laura, by the way, tell me yours later. None of them do and he's done it before. No, it was the Dermot-wrangling that I was being asked to do. I'd not been asked to drag him out of anywhere yet; and had been glad. Many had, and from what I'd heard he hadn't been amenable to any kind of coaxing in most situations unless it was near the end of the day's shoot, when he'd be as nice as he could be – which wasn't much and then it was because, we found, that he'd usually be able to give his minders the slip and scuttle off somewhere to sit in a bar on his own for a while. I guess decades of practice has given him a nose for these things. A somewhat reddened one, from what I've seen. Gives make-up something to do, although as he's employed to be the archetypal old throwback Id've thought they could leave that in. What's the point of sanitising the satanic?

Yes, that's the real core of it, the real reason all the strata above me had shirked the chance to walk with history and bring him to whatever mark was needed. And why they were all stood about obviously waiting for me to do the thing I'd been commanded to do.

There's something else about that man. He's not right. It's like he's haunted. By something, or just actually haunted himself. In the way that houses are, supposedly, you know? Don't go near that house, it's haunted, someone says, and you think, yeah it looks like it. Well don't go near that man, it's a haunted man. Oh god yes, I think I can see something moving in the eye sockets.

People started to avoid him in the second week. It got around, he hadn't exactly done anything but he always had the atmosphere around him that something was going to happen, something was near snapping. And no-one could detect what, nothing anyone was doing to cause it, seemingly, just a deep glower out at everything. Seeing stuff around him, in us, that wasn't really there? Something old, deep, buried back in that skull.

There's something going on in there, alright. I've seen him when he's between takes and I'm between tasks. Sat alone, not quite muttering to himself but more not quite alone with himself. Not especially wanting to be with anyone, lest of all this flotilla of berks; but always seeming as if he's turning something over in his mind, putting off something that he's headed to. Look, I'm not too experienced in dealing with older types, at least the ones I'm not related to and I'm used to them. But this is an old actor, a definite old-school actor. And we all know that even the sanest of actors aren't quite right, really. Our Dermot was from a generation of anti-public relations, where the fights he got into and the people he knocked into Shaftesbury Avenue were part of the publicity they used. That's what I heard from Director of Photography, when he was holding forth to some nubiles over lunch. Having seen that face of his, I don't doubt it. It's ruined, like an all-over scar. Bony, cutting cheekbones jutting out, with deep set but piercing eyes that I haven't had trained on me and don't want, thanks. Baleful, wounded intent is the look. I can see why they chose him, train a camera on that and people would read in years of regret. But one of the positives about actors is their ability to convey everything without having that actually going on in their heads. I wonder if that's true of this character.

So I accepted my commission – yeah, not much else I could do. The wind was getting up, and we had light left for enough time to get one shoot left, in other words not enough for me to hesitate. I didn't say anything, just padded my way over to the little narrow tent he'd been put in for safety. I could see a smirk or two from those around David, our director. Ok, my turn.

I could hear low muttering as I neared the tent, something threading through the whipping noise of the wind. How long he'd been there I didn't know but I expected that it would be too long for him, despite being on set with the crew being a far worse option for him. He's surely have heard me by now, perhaps seen a silhouette. It's normal – no, needed- to give a door a knock before you give someone their call. You know the reputation these people have, you never know what they might be getting up to and let's face it they probably are.

Never having knocked on a tent before, I froze for a moment. That's when he gave a growl of acknowledgement. I'd been seen and he knew it was time. But, just in case (of what, I now think? Him being caught sacrificing crabs?) I said –

-We're ready, Mr Boyle, Scene 14.

Another husky thrum boomed out below the wind. This one could have almost been a word. I opened the tent, and he was already creaking up. I mean, he was starting to stand and I swear he was creaking with the effort. He was cocooned in several layers of old stuff –tweed, mostly, and by the look of him the little heater had kept some kind of pulse moving. He put out his elbow for balance and I took it. We had about thirty feet to walk and although I was dry-throated at the prospect of aiding this wraith, I didn't want him breaking or billowing off into the sea on my watch. If getting a tea order wrong got me screamed at I couldn't imagine what killing one of the leads would get me in. He was thin, alright, I could feel that his arm was frighteningly thin – could be near mine, but I had no sense of frailty. Makes sense considering what happened soon afterward.

I took his elbow and we walked across the sand, with the crew looking over intently. The wind was against us but we were both leaning into it. For someone who looked so frail he was flinching far less than me. I was still wary of making conversation, so was glad that the noise of the wind precluded any effort of doing so, although what would I have said apart from asking about how his tent was, I don't know. I could see that he was on the periphery of conversing with himself – muttering something indistinct to himself, although whether it was about the situation he was approaching or something imagined, something from his past, I couldn't know.

Within a minute or two we were there and as soon as we were, the continuity and make up people got to him and I peeled off to my usual place on the periphery. Throughout this process of buffing and prepping he was utterly still, allowing the girls to dust his face off and order his eyebrows, whilst continuity fiddled with his lapels. All the while those eyes were set somewhere far off, visualising somewhere he couldn't return to but wanted to be, it seemed. Or maybe one of the bars in town. Due to utter concentration or complete inertia he didn't seem to move at all, the only reaction I noticed was a growled comment after David had started to give a note, I didn't hear it but I heard a couple of the techies laughing so guessed it was something rude, and probably something about Hero or David himself. I guessed because I could see David clamming up and chewing his lip, the poor lamb, having no idea what to do. Dermot smirked and raised a hand, seemingly a signal that whatever he said should be discarded and he was ready to work.

Now, at this point I hadn't seen the old stick doing any work up close. I'd mostly seen Zephiah and The Drip bollocking through their little scenarios, which was so boring in itself that I tended to drift away and see what was going on off set, as it was invariably more interesting than anything being attempted near the cameras.

He didn't have much to do for this scene – from what I'd read of the ever-changing script it seemed to be a reaction shot of him walking a few paces and freezing as he remembers something his daughter's said. The voiceover would be doing most of the work, with its internal monologue needlessly spelling out what the audience would hopefully have construed for themselves. So, I was essentially looking at an old bloke moving hesitantly and pausing.

What I saw was profound. I know I wasn't alone, as I checked with the boom afterward. He said,

-Yes, weird, isn't it. It's like he's barely there, then when the take happens, it isn't just that he's in the moment of the scene, but something deeper is happening, something is opening up within himself. It's, dunno, like when we have the cameras on him some other man, who-

-Who's more alive?

-Yes, and we somehow see what he's thinking, we're drawn in. Whereas outside of that –

-No-one's home.

-Yes, or if there is, you wouldn't want to meet him.

That, friend, is the nearest I've got to having a poetic conversation on this set. Not that it even got close to the weirdness I felt, it was like the man himself hadn't a clue that it was happening, something unconsciously switched on as soon as the cameras were rolling; and it wasn't just a different person inhabiting that tired vessel, but one that was more present, more real, than the haunted thing we worked with otherwise.

The boom guy, again-

-Well, you can actually see why he was hired now, can't you?

Yes, I could. But, see, the other side of this rusty coin is that the effect of this other person vanishing when the day's shooting was over was all the more disquieting, all the more disturbing. Suddenly he was diminished, crumpled back into blank eyed insolence. Where had the other gone? Did he even realise that it had happened? If he was switching this thing on and off, was he deliberately holding something back when interacting with the rest of us, or was this something that welled up from within the recesses of that desiccated husk involuntarily, without any effort or input from his conscious self?

Well, how could we know? The person that was left behind after the work was over gave every impression of wanting to elude the pool of humanity around him, and we were happy to oblige. It was easy enough for him to do, I guess, amongst a large amount of people who were trying to elude each other anyway. But it was still chilling to see the inner animation vanish within seconds of cut being called. Clouded over. Like a little death, for want of a better phrase. I remember them, all right. Can't remember how long...

Anyway, turns out that was the day when he decked the priest. See what I mean? I was first on the scene, albeit accidentally. God, why would I have wanted to turn up to see that deliberately? It was truly sordid. The poor padre had just wed a compromised looking couple of middle-agers, the reception was in the hotel we'd shacked Dermot in, and they'd been so happy with the day that they'd invited the priest back to sup some non-holy wine. He'd been leaving the reception when Dermot came in, moving as fast and with as much intent as he can, having been supping alone for an hour or two. The sight must have been truly alarming, even without the resulting punch. Like Dracula being fired out of a cannon. Either way, something in that weird, desiccated mind had focused on our priest, who I'm guessing before his face was split would have seemed to have a rather pleasant look to him. Perhaps that set him off? Either way, he ended the day with an open face in the literal sense.

This was when most of us realised that something was awry with the man. Not because he lashed out at a blameless target, drunkenly. Not so much. More the fact that he addressed the victim by his own name. He didn't seem to know where he started and ended. Dermot against Dermot.

That's a mean, cock-snapper of a wind whipping up and around this little tent. Straight into the balls it goes. If I can feel this I must be awake, and to be awake, I must still be alive, against all the evidence. Feeling pain in my balls is the only proof I have that I'm still there. The wind has been bringing sand through up through the tight little apertures and right into the few openings the big woolly coat has been allowing. Cold. Shivery. Still morning I'm guessing, it's probably hours that I've been sat here half dead on this wobbly fold-up chair, myself sinking into the ground as what little weight I have is sucked into the wet sand.

Hours. When would they be ready for the short time I'll be needed, needed to just stand there and gaze back up toward the shore as if I'm thinking of something? In France they'd have had wine ready for me, well, they did in the sixties, himself remembers that alright. Even if I'd tended not to remember the rest of each day's work after the warm wine had gone down. But I hadn't needed to remember, didn't need to know, I'd made stuff that made memories for the world, cherished memories. Of moments that had never happened.

Wine. God, I'd murder a little warm pot of it now. France was wine, England is pissy coffee, prissily given. Look down at your feet now, by the wellies, down indented in the sand, still got the little Styrofoam cup there? Yup, one of the weightless little white fellas where I'd left him, screwed into the tide- dampened sand for safekeeping. A little left? Yes, I've a little oily deposit of black stuff, not vinous alas but there has to be appreciable caffeine to glug up, better than a mouthful of air, which is all I'll have otherwise. So bend down, reach my left arm out, ah yes still a southpaw after all these years, clamp the bony owl claw over it. Reach, damn me, reach it back up, hard to manoeuvre under all these necessary layers. Yes, got it, waveringly it's brought up, bring it to the withered old gob, at least my mouthhole can't age, it'll take stuff as greedily as it did all the other years.

Tepid altogether, tasteless murk just as I'd feared. Hold it in the gob now, let it sluice around the toothless gaps there, got to be good for a bit of vim of a morning, if not well I'll pass the time by doing so. That's enough now, time to swallow the bugger, one gobful is that's all that's left but all that I'll be getting till I shout. Down. Not even a warmth in the throat. Look at me here in my tent, just a little bit bigger than myself, and with all my layers almost filling it up. Holding a Styrofoam cup and downing the contents like I'm some mad earl taking the first oyster of the season whilst sniffing the sea air. Cold as that would be, my murk, slithering down the throat. Better not think of oysters mind, it'll make me want to heave up anything I have down in the gizzard.

Is there anything? Anything last night? No idea. Earlier this morning? Again, I ask myself, are we still there in the morning? Ah yes, some bacon roll or two. They were good enough to have them ready on a winter's morning, I'd have turned back had they not and you know they would have all followed me too.

Long day ahead of me, I think. And god knows it keeps going, receding away from me. I still have the cup in my hand, why? Let the bloody thing go down to the ground, it'll go nowhere. Eh? Another gust through that blasted aperture and it's blown up, upended and it's levitated up to the narrow top of my plastic little tepee. Insolent as well as tasteless and useless. Well let it stay there. It'll do no better anywhere else.

Waving as quick as I can go, keep the airborne sand from my eyes. No good, I'm far slower than the wind nowdays, the sand is all over the shop and I'm just waving to myself like some mad regal muppet. And no-one to see. Well, let it go on, too much effort to break the motion now and if anyone opens the tent I'll look daft but haven't I been found doing worse? And when do I not look daft nowdays anyways?

All the layers, six? Seven? Coddling my scrawny body and if its all keeping me warm I'm none the wiser. Down at the heavy wellies, feet encased in two pairs of thick socks within, and am I imagining the water getting in anyways? For future reference –may be drowning on this bloody job.

What about the rest? Two coats, jumpers, lumberjack get up, must look bulky and warm but I feel like a skinny fella that's been eaten by some fat fuck and is politely waiting to digest. Why anyone'd gobble me up, I'm not so sure, apart from to tell the story afterward, 'Yes you remember him, well I ate the lot of him and he was no better than a stick of dry spaghetti.'

Better quell these morbid thoughts. Won't get me through the day well. Not until they have more food to throw at us, at the least. What's this coat? Big tweedy greatcoat, Sherlock style, not mine I'll tell meself that. Like something straight from the props cupboard, collar up so I'm making like Bela Lugosi with his cape, folded up for extra mystery. Bet I look very mysterious now, the enigma being, why is that old fella wrapped up in that tent for hours on a beach? Still need the lucre, despite my years, that's why, me dears.

Sad, really. Still, who'd take a comfy armchair retirement over this? Quell the thought of the comfy armchair there, no point of thinking about one unless they can stuff one in here with you. And there's no room and no budget.

Now let's see, space...raise those arms out, in their tweedy sleeves. Took a while but I have time on my hands. My hands at the tarpaulin, either side, yes I can fill my empire with one stretch of the arms.

Like a massive tweedy penguin. Concentric, like the tent I'm trapped in, come to think of it. Like its grown out of me. They could do with some tweedy penguins round here. It'd lift the mood, and they'd fit right in. Spending my last days on a grey beach with grey sand blowing in my mush. Well, always a game of snakes and ladders, with more of one than the other.

I wonder if my time of popping off has happened already. Is this a cold purgatory, or the worse place...could be, for a starter. Wouldn't be going up anywhere else, would I now.

Eh? What was that thought? No idea. Start again. I must move, even if they don't need me. Where are they? Can hear distant noise of bollocks being spouted. As ever. How far? Sounds like far away up the beach there, and oh god if there's any new food and it hasn't been brought I'll strangle them with this tent. Wind up again, more salt coming through the crack for my no doubt rheumy eyes.

Busted flush here, may as well move out. Creak yourself up now, hold on to the stool even though this old thing I'm living in is as light as some stretched bird skeleton, slowly, but I'm up-and I can look out, yes, feeling steady in my wellies. God, the sun's further down than I thought, beaming out behind me and making the shore and the clumpy little town behind it look almost lovely. Ghosts of sand racing down toward it, coming off the sea, am I imagining some of them as figures that stand still for a second –snap – and then whip themselves away, dissolving even quicker as they dissipate toward the land, nearer that desperate crew over there?

God they look pooped out. I'd forgotten that young people get tired too. My influence, no doubt. Well, perhaps it's that I'm difficult to work with, I've heard it said, even by those who still talk to me (and I think they're still alive). Or is it just that the sight of me reminds them of what's coming and takes the life out of them? If they're lucky?

Far away enough to be a shivery tableau of petrified gnomes, ruddy enough cheeks I'm imagining. Both sets. Some kind of argument going on about the spindly equipment, the light stands, the big reflecting yoke to catch the light and bring out the reflectee's eyes, I used to remember what the blasted thing was called. Go on, let it all sink into these sands, let's call it a day for god's sake and get me back into the warmth where I don't have to glide about like some mad fat lummox. Six weeks done. I know it'll be my last. And I know I should be relishing it, holding every day to savour as a memory for the rest of my senescence, but, look –those of us who make a living from doing this; even we get the heebie jeebies once in a while about how fecking ridiculous it is to get paid for being pretend. The pretend self always more convincing than the banal, normal reality. People still don't believe that I have to go to the frozen food isle like everyone else for my weekly feed. And even though I know it's the last time, and many others never even get asked when they hit their whatever decade (which decade am I on? I'll recall when I've defrosted, later). But here, look at the state of me and look where I am – would you be surprised if I wasn't tinged with shame?

Stood looking, I think they have noticed. Glad to be standing by my self and everything but dear God where have my balls gone? I have only a slight sensation of most of myself in this tweed pyramid around me, and none whatsoever of my nadgers. Please –please let them still be there. The more I get toward the end, the more my belief in god and my balls becomes intertwined. I'm hoping for some sensation of them being there as the days go by, but I'm losing faith in finding either party. And yet, thinking back over the years, I knew they were both there at some point. They've just deserted me of late. I'll never find them in all this sand.

Here comes one –oh, a girl. Small mercies. I can see the rictus smile from here, she's no more enjoying the trudge than I would, but she's here on a mission. Prise the salty old oyster out of his shell, that's the designated mission. I'll be happily obliged if you're doing the pulling, gal. Just hope there's something left in there.

So here I am in my sinking wellies, had better look primed and ready for another take, or several hours of takes, jeezus I'm feeling more tired thinking about it. Just think about those bright lamps warming one up as the others huddle round their equipment, whilst freezing their own private equipment off.

She's closer. What's my face doing? React, damn you, it's your job, it's what keeps the rest of this body in beers and fags! Look ready. Look focused. Ah no, something's happening in the cheeks, they're flexing, the effort's knackering me out already. I can see it in her nearing eyes, I must be leering, albeit inadvertently, the face does that when I'm trying to look smiley and debonair nowdays, well not much I can do about that, surely it's better than remaining in saggy old poker face mode. Hm, maybe not, I think I can see some fear growing in her eyes now, resentment at having to be the one to get the old crab out of the shell. Well, can I blame her.

She's spouting something, it's lost in the wind and the sand but I know the gist either way. Its time to get in position, ready at the mark.

-I'll need a hand or two, I'm stuck in the sand here, I'm saying before I know it, although all I hear is a long dry honk projecting itself over the beach at her. She understands it alright, she's coming over to take me. Please, take me by the arm as best you can, although I can see that you're struggling with this sea-bog as well. Nothing like a bit of slapstick to warm one up before work. I still can't remember if her name's Rachelle or Rochelle or Roy but I'm good with making the R's at the start of my sentence before going on so that she knows I'm talking to her and appreciates that I remember her name. Senescence has been kind to me in that way, I never have to make the effort anymore because no-one thinks I'm able to. Ostentatiously remember that you've met the person before – even if it was yesterday - and you're well away.

And so I am, she's got the furry penguin's flipper in her arm and we're both waddling with intent toward the site. Fast as we can, which isn't fast at all, though given how I feel like a gust of that sandy wind could lift me into a trajectory over the beach and into the north sea, my tweed billowing out behind me, I'm thinking I should be paid double for this.

-Oye-feele-oye-shud-bee-paaayd dubble-fer-dhissss-

She's looking quizzically over at me. Shite. I actually said it there, didn't I. Not made any easier by the wind rattling my flesh clear away from my skull, it felt like, but not bad as far as the first hello of the day to the crew goes.

And here they are. An overjoyed-looking crew, I must say. Fiddling with their equipment (the electrical kind, although given half a chance and a warm room I wouldn't put it past them) and barely a look up to acknowledge the minor miracle of me having trudged over without falling down and breaking my arse on the sand.

-Good morning Dermot, sorry to have kept you. We've got about an hour maximum to get this, it's just a cut-away so its a few seconds, but this is the pivotal one we were talking about last time-

I do recall, as it was yesterday. My looks have died but my brain hasn't, you daft little scrote.

He's looking crestfallen, all of a sudden. And the crew are slyly laughing –giving that look I've gotten used to over the last few weeks, the one that only comes in my direction. Shit. Said it out loud, didn't I. Well, it's happened before and it'll happen again.

-So yes, I'm ready, I should say. Still, he's the director and he should be able to endure my little idiosyncrasies.

And as soon as I'm there the blusher and powder is out to tart me up for the public. Lipstick on a cadaver, may as well be. If I'm not gone by the time the film ever comes out – if it ever comes out – they'll be watching mainly to say, ah remember him? I thought he'd gone already, god not long until he does. And if they remember me, they'll be of the departure lounge age too. People of a younger hue –this lot, come to think of it – won't have a clue and they won't want to have a clue.

Well yeah, that's if it's ever finished, or ever released, or if any fecker deigns to watch it. Not fussed, either way. Just so long as they money comes in. I'm a professional to the end. I do this as a job, don't give two hoots about seeing films, especially ones I'm in, they're bound to be bad. As bad as it was to make them. Yes, think of the money. Had better not die before those checks clear or I'll never enjoy it.

-And cut! Good.

What the biscuit? Yes, it was the mimsy young shite saying it. Damn it, I daydreamed through my first take of the day.

-I think that was pretty perfect, we'll do a couple for luck now.

We'd better do one I'm conscious of, for a starter, you privileged little foetus of a fecker. If I don't mind? No, we're definitely doing more. I think I can remember what I was meant to do, even though I seem to have just done it anyways. Christ, I'll never get it right now I know I'm supposed to be doing it.

Cut – if you can look in the same direction as last time, please.

Here we go. Now where was I?

Cut, ok can wardrobe please come in, and continuity? The costume has...ah, come free..

Something I'm aware of, thanks, due to the cold, no need to snigger; I wasn't going to try and adjust myself when we were rolling, was I? Fuck it, I won't say anything. On with the endurance. I've noticed that Bosch isn't here, with his old man's beard on a young shite's face, so I'm grateful for this small mercy amongst the sand blasted endurance. They think I'm oblivious to how things have gone here, but I can tell just how much he's hated by nearly all present. They're positively chipper, despite being huddled on a bleak beach in an English seaside town, helping a desiccated old actor repeating himself for money.

I've seen some bad behaviour on sets over my decades. Mostly created by myself, but I've noticed others doing it and there's different strata of oafishness. An actor like me, never quite such a big bollocks that the money was following him, the fuck-you money that meant you could get people fired rather than being over the trap door yourself, well our kind could have our moments between takes, snapping at the director of photography or getting up to something near the honeywagon, yes. But we never had underlings, not our level of power. This fella- the producer – well, I'm getting the impression that he's viewing the entire town as his grateful lickspittles, let alone his subordinate crew.

You see, he's been conditioned to expect everything from everyone and he's in a context where it'll have to happen or the poor shite in the crosshairs will be fired and blacklisted. Sayonara to the beautiful career you've busted a gut to get to. I'm used to that, nothing new, over the decades, it's more that my tolerance for this kind of drip decreases the older I get and the younger they get.

This one, despite having the facial hair of a hermit, underneath all that fuzz probably doesn't look old enough to shave. I keep expecting to see an umbilical cord trailing around his chunky ankles.

And posh. Oh god, the poshness. He looks like he's never had to wipe his own arse, let alone cook for himself. I can't tolerate anyone having people swarming around them doing things for them that they can't do themselves.

Oh god, the poshness. The loud poshness. When did everyone in this game get posh? I don't mind it being a young person's game, everyone on earth is younger than me so it's the way it has to be. But most of this crew speak in accents that my lot had to learn for the kind of roles that we weren't supposed to get but people loved us for getting. Yes, and between takes we'd use our real voices to speak to the crew, sparkies who'd been on the job since Gainsborough Studios time and knew their way around every other soundstage in the country. This bunch, even that sultry runner, they don't look like they've had an underfed month in their short lives. And the town don't like them. I've taken it in, I see people raising their heads toward the young lungs bellowing out unnecessarily; they're starting to crumple inwardly at the sight of the parade of them. Six weeks we've been here, and they're yet to get used to them.

Especially Bosh, our Hero. No, not in that sense, he's the producer – did I not tell you yet? Yes, I know, makes him all the more loathsome, him being called Hero. I've always thought that nominative determinism is a load of cobblers. Look here though, we have it in negative form, whatever beasts birthed this wally bequeathed him such a self-regarding name, inviting such egocentrism, that he was bound to end up being the polar opposite of a hero.

'Ok, folks, we're done for the day. Dermot, thanks, especially. Dermot?'

I'm taken aback. Since I've been on my little rant, it seems that I've completed a few more takes successfully. I told you, the less you think about it, the better you get. I meant the acting but that can also go for the ranting. I haven't even said thanks to the director (now what's his name again?), seem to have just given a semi-regal wave and hobbled on my way. With the help. The director is certainly giving his thanks on eggshells, probably because of whatever I may have done the other night. Well, whatever I may have got up to, some air needed clearing.

I know what's coming up now, and so do they. I'll be escorted to the hotel room, and I'll give them the slip. The great thing about looking like you need help to get through a door is that people are always underestimating your ability to unobtrusively disappear. Well, provided there's a quiet bar to be found. And there is, I know them all now. And they seem to tolerate me. It isn't the sullen runner taking me today, it seems, shame as there seems to be something interesting and human ratting around her sarky young skull. But I can see that she's laden down with tea cups and detritus today. Instead I've got the wobbly faced young fellow, pastry-faced rather than pasty given the weather, but he'll be easy work to get away from. Here, take my arm you daft young pup, don't look so bloody tired and afraid. I'll be away from you soon.

Now here we go, we're in the town and there's a few more people walking around, I can feel the sundown starting behind me and I know the route to both where I'm supposed to be going (hotel) and where I will be getting (pub). The trick is an easy one for my type, and one that is evergreen. I'm starting to imagine something alarming and large, you see, and am starting to visualise it in my mind, shaping it in three dimensions, breathing life into it. Can you see it too? Bit bull-like, no? Perhaps a bit of elephant, yes. Let's expand it a bit, anything to make it more startling, until it's crystal-clear in my mind, and then-

Yes-

There it is a bold as bollocks, ten feet away from us in a shop doorway. Now, I know that I'm reacting to its presence and because of this the young fellow next to me will be too –yes, there he is, looking where I'm looking – and the second he's turned away I've slipped my skeletal arm out of his shaky grasp and tottered down an alleyway to my left, which leads to my intended destination.

I'm on the bar stool and have a pint in my grasp within minutes. Finishing with the last light of day like this, I'll have a good hour or so before the pubs get too busy, not that I think this one will, but I've timed them and the average countdown to find me is one hour twenty minutes. How wonderfully hapless they are.

I like this pub. Its wonderfully forgotten. It has burgundy curtains, half-frosted glass and yellowed walls. Not sure if they're painted yellow or just yellowed down from some other, purer, colour. Well, they are where they are now, which is nice and putrid. But look down, and take a gander at the scuffed majesty below. This carpet seems to have set up home here in the seventies and has no intention of being moved. It's hard to ignore, at least for people like me who are attracted to things whose time is nearly up. It's the colour of a particularly worrying vomit, swirls of yellow and deep red mixing together like the last of an unfortunate's bile, trodden into permanence. Yes, very seventies. In fact, I do wonder if I'm drawn to it – feels like I'm literally attached to it at present -because, I realise now, it's set my thoughts off to the carpet of a green room I knew regularly in that decade, may even be the same design, I can't tell, but now the memories are becoming more vivid than the world as it is in front of me and we're off-

I'm being interviewed by some bouffant with corduroy, sometime in the early seventies, trickle of sweat running down the far left of my forehead, the pukey patchwork of the audiences' clothes made especially arresting by being suspended in the black box of the studio. Not my first TV interview as myself, but I'm remembering this as I'm smoking and drinking during it. God, strange to think we could do that, even encouraged. Few in the green room beforehand with some singing girl and a motorcyclist that drove through bales of hay for money. I don't remember them chuffing away during the interview, but I needed it. Something had started to slip, this is when I've just fallen out of youth and hit early middle age, the bouffant is asking me what I think of the younger men who have appeared all around me and taken the roles I've been used to.

I've been piffling away his obvious attempt to bate me with blandishments, but he knows that this can only go so far. I've lost a quarter of my yearly income to these little shits, which is partly why I'm on the chat show circuit and that's certainly why I've been asked to appear in the first place. I'm on the skids somewhat and they know it. Love it.

Now the host has asked a follow-up question and I can only bat these away for so long, I can feel the audience's collective anticipation, they don't want any more of this politesse and there's a definite sense that if something doesn't snap they'll lose interest. Now, even though I have a degree of dignity to defend here, and I don't want to let all know just how annoying it is - how the host's needling has got to me, there is a higher law here that I must respect, and that is to not bore my audience. They must not lose interest.

I'm saying something bland to fill the air, but as I'm doing so I can feel that something is different and I can see something switch in the presenter's eyes. He's essentially been on autopilot over the last half hour, working through what he needed to do, but he hasn't had any surprises to deal with yet. He's done a subtle, inadvertent double-take which lets me know that not only has something unexpected cropped up, he knows that it's good, and the hundred or so people in this sweaty black box have sat up, engaged.

The voice I'm speaking with is no longer mine. And everyone in the studio knows who it belongs to. It's one of the younger turks the bouffant has mentioned, an unmistakeably cockney tone that's made him stand out against the competition, and its standing out here as everyone knows what I'm doing. I'm throwing this fella's success back at the presenter. I don't need to name him, I'm simply becoming him, as I can do that if I so wish.

I know I've got them hooked now, all of them, and in one ghastly moment I realise that I'm overstepping it. Most of the people who come on the show can probably do this, there's mimics in many actors, and they let them loose, sometimes, but away from the cameras. Away from the thousands, no millions, possibly, this is happening when all people had to do was watch TV. And away from the contemporary who, if not watching then, would find out soon enough and hear everything.

The look. The look in the interviewer's eyes says it. He knows he's got gold dust out of me, but I'm doing it at my cost. And you know, now that I remember it again, crystal, clear as the Jameson in my glass then and now, I know that I've been baited and sunk to the occasion.

But I can't stop it. No, the voice is coming out and I know I'm saying something he would, spot on, I've seen and sublimated him over the years of knowing he was coming up my outside flank. It's its own thing now and I'm a vessel that's unable to cork it when I know it's too late already. That's the dangerous thing about having this kind of chaotic stuff bubbling within you, you can call upon it but when the damned buzzing thing within gets the opportunity to get out – to get the air that it needs to feed, the laughs, the outraged intake of breath from the audience – you can't stop it. It might decide. The floor director may cut it off. But you, the golem it's speaking through, you have no recourse to quell it. It's pitiless, this mysterious thing, and we'll all tell you that the both brilliant and pant-wettingly sordid thing about it is, the sensation is that of being truly out-of-control.

The director or one of the others up in the lit room with the table mikes must be blathering in the presenter's ear, he's managed to take control and is talking to the young one, taking the spotlight away from whatever the hell I've been doing. I can feel the audience shuffling and murmuring to themselves, they have the release of knowing that my nasty little homunculus is back in his bottle. The driddle of sweat that was on my brow has now joined some of its friends in the folds of my velvet shirt, joining up to course down my back.

-Well, thank you Dermot, or should I say Dermot and Larry. Tell me Samantha, you had the pleasure of working with Dermot when he was just himself recently, how did you find him?

Quiet, flat, nonchalant, but also cutting, her reply-

-Yeah, he's hilarious.

A laugh from the audience, in unison now, a laugh of relief. Order is restored. I don't remember the rest.

A day later, in my agent's office. She said-

-You got all of us talking.

Me, slumped in the little room, sweating like billyo again even though no lights are on, the window is open onto a breezy Charing Cross Road.

-Dermot, you took the bait. Why?

God knows what I said. I knew when summoned that this would be a trouble meeting. A discussion. I was trying not to shake.

-You know that they do that kind of thing and you know that they love seeing it get to people, especially when it's someone who's not at the top any more.

Yes, we both knew that. My demon had certainly known it. And what I'd done had changed things, greased my grip on the little perch I had. Bad me. As ever.

-The others and I have talked. We still want to keep you, but it's best if you keep a quieter profile for a while.

Sitting between us, almost instantly yellowing newspaper stories of the thing, and the occasional curt but dignified retort from the man I mimicked. Oh, the trouble I'd sown.

I have some ideas about portmanteau films for some of the production companies here, and there are American series shooting, but until I can prove you're not a liability – considering how interested this lot have been in your off-camera jollies with those fists of yours-I'll be holding off putting you up for what we've had recently. You weren't a story unto yourself back then, Dermot. No, I know you're listening, Dermot, but listen closer–remember this. We'll keep you on. But you need to behave. This is work, a job, not everything is performance art. Or piss art. If you can't get that in your head, bear in mind that your forties are already well on you. Listen deeply to what I'm saying and get your brain around it, or you'll forever remember this as when you left success behind and the skids started calling.

And remember I do, as through frosted glass. Oh, the decades between then and now, they're nothing. Distended reflection of the pub carpet in my glass. A breeze from the open door behind me tells me it's them, I don't even need to check the barman's look or turn around. Glass back on the bar, I put up my hands in supplication–caught! Bedtime for Bonzo, I'm guessing.

And a young exhalation behind me tells me I'm right.

Two hours later, in a darker, smarter room, two younger men were talking at each other.

-No, look, the insurance is fine and we'll be in no trouble on that front, he'll make it through the shoot. It's just the rest of us I'm piqued about. Can we make it along with him?

This was the larger one, who had relaxed himself into a long leather armchair. An explosion of beard covered his face from the nostrils down and was so dense that it gave the impression that any noise coming from the mouth occlued within would surely be muffled at best. But the voice was not only clear, it was loud, piping, and far too steady for someone who had been awake for nineteen hours.

-I don't get it.

-I don't get it either, but it's happened.

-Was he drunk?

-Ever seen him sober?

-It's hard to tell, sometimes I wonder if he's acting it to make us think he can't take directon.

-Well, he frequently doesn't.

-He'll need some now. Into an isolation booth.

-Right. Is he ok, that's the main thing.

-Is he ok, he did the punching, why are you asking if he's the one left ok? It's the innocent priest we should be talking about here.

-We'll get to the priest in time. The priest is fine from what I hear, I'm asking about Dermot because with the way he moves usually I'd imagine that lifting his own right arm above chest hight would give him a coronary, let along giving someone a wallop. And he's the lead, no matter what Zephiah thinks. Just don't tell her that. We're nowhere near enough finished to recast, even if his right arm falls off.

The other man, who was less bearded and less loud, at this point started to run through the film's remaining shooting schedule in his mind, trying to calculate if his lead actor had any scenes needing the use of his right arm, or indeed any limb, and if so how he would be able to shoot around the loss of one or any of the spindly attachments. He answered his producer, quite in earnest –

-It was still attached to the rest of him, that's the last I heard. And yes, I wouldn't have believed it had I not seen the result. Some of the hotel staff were openly weeping, I don't think they see much action in these parts. There was blood and vom on the carpet.

-It's a good thing he isn't famous anymore or we'd have to be in PR overdrive.

-And that'd be a quarter of our budget out the window.

-Half. At least no one is going to press charges. But we'll need to move him to another hotel.

-Surely every hotel in town will know about this now?

-They do, but we'll pay more. That, we can afford. And he'll be on his best behaviour. He'll be looked after properly.

The quieter man, the director, reached for his bottle of beer. They had almost finished both of theirs. Four more empties were on the table. As he lifted his up he realised that his fidgeting had stopped. His body was too tired. He said, feeling his tongue heavy within his mouth-

-What set him off this time, anyway? Normally it's just shouting.

-I don't know, no-one does and that seems to include him. It is scary, David. I mean scarier than him getting the black cloud and either going shouty or silent, even with the violence, there's something else. Laura was first on the scene, and she said that he was raving and drooling, but both she and the priest that went down said that he was referring to the priest as Dermot. Himself.

-He'd mistaken someone for himself?

-Hmm.

-So where did that leave him?

-Too late for the existential question, I'm afraid. Not that I'd know.

-Look. Really. Are we really all safe here?

-We're safe, I'll make us safe. He's crossed-or-punched his way across a line, but he knows it. No-one is going to die. At least, not while we have all this to finish in two weeks. There will be no false moves. He can't afford to screw it up, who'll have him now? And he needs us, remember.

-Owl scene on Saturday. Will his arm take it?

-I think we can have the owl on either left or right arm. But I'll check on that. Night, bozo.

It's when I'm left alone that I know I'm truly damned. Oh, I'm alone with everybody, alright. I might well be ignoring all I can, but that doesn't mean that I don't need them around me.

Something's opening up beneath me, jaws prised open and ready to swallow. Gaping maw. Black. I can try to push the realisation away from the front of what's left of my mind when I'm out in the world, but there's nothing to stop it when its just me and the walls, here.

I know that I will die soon, if not dead already, and I am due an almighty reckoning. When I think back to what I can remember of my life, I can't think what this would be for as there's simply too many options. Decades of shame. Botches, brawl-rattled wives and constant betrayals. Now, look, I've had the displeasure of reading my own obituary, and it wasn't pretty. I didn't mind the essential failure of the whole enterprise, it was the sense of a continued self indulgence wrecking myself and all within orbit.

I hadn't thought of my life like that. I'd been looking away from whatever wreckage was left behind me, in constant motion. But being dictated to by my own damn whims. Oh, I'd known I'd failed in many things, not least the work that I set out to do, but when I saw it in black and white I realised that I'd been ruining more than myself over the decades. Damage. I have provoked damage in every petty little endeavour I've set out on. If I could just bring it all upon myself...

And now there is no time. Nothing left now. Apart from me in the dark listening to the rain pissing itself against the window. Fair soundtrack to the last days of a piss artist who should have known better. During the day I can suppress the fear, the certainty that this is the end of my time, in the day, whilst amongst the others. Barely suppressed, but motion can do that to you, it's what I did over my lifetime, keep in motion, moving on, away from the differing wreckages I've created. Strewn.

There isn't much motion left in me now. Can't they see it in my eyes? Surely it's seeping out? God, the one time I really recognise tasting fear in my life and they're all blind to it. Not that they're an audience. Maybe they are, not that they know it.

Freshly suppressed during the day, roaring back as soon as I'm alone at night. I can't forget it even at the peak of day though, bubbling away there. I can't forget all the instances of screams and blood and retributions down the years, there's no distance between us now to make them memories. They aren't, they're ganging up at the periphery of my vision, god help me what will I see when these furies are in full view? Oh, never alone with you all. Do I wonder if I'm starting to see you in the daylight, with your calm beseeching blank faces staring right out at me? I can't look back at you, I can't meet your gaze. Maybe if I do that'll be the end of it and you'll just rush up to me and I'll finally cut out, like a knackered bulb-

No. No, don't give up and don't get hysterical. Your obituary, it had no date that you saw, old dog. It's piling up on top of you, but don't invite the blackout yet. If I could spend most of my time fighting to kick start myself back to life again perhaps this is the time I really need to keep up the habit. Hold yourself close now. That thing, out there, looking at you in the darkness, you know it's real, as real as anything in the grey day. Just keep your steel. Don't let people know you're living in a state of terror.

Oh god how weird it is to be spending the last days of freedom with the youngest crew I've ever seen. Scrotes and jailbait, all. Is this your way of mocking me? Fine, I'd find myself funny if I didn't have to be me.

The barely adult. And someone has asked for me, sent for me to be in this? I don't know how I'm doing it. Really, the young have a different register, we can barely hear each other. And when I do make out the occasional phrase it makes little or no sense to me, or whatever makes sense is asinine piffle. Well, the young. They make you feel extra old. Surrounded by the barely sentient when I'm erasing inwardly.

They're still swimming at the side of my eyes, you know. I know that I'm sat here on the edge of a bed in a hotel, between movements, doing nothing but trying to avoid my thought and own sight. I can't even rest my gaze on the grey reflection in the window. I don't want to see that saggy old dog expression any more than I want to look at the empty old eyebags. Stay like this until sleep comes. Fine, then they'll call. Another day away from it.

Fine. It's work. I'll die working? Good.

Y'know, I'm not sure if I'll ever get out of this rut, but look on the positives -I can still remember how I got here. And why I did. Blundering promise. Talent! Blazing talent! For doing whatever I wasn't supposed to be doing at the time. And what I was supposed to be doing at the time was a degree in something that definitely wasn't film-making. It wasn't history, literature or social theory either, although it did tend to say it was all of those things. Where it was was in a University on the flat edge of West London that had way too much concrete for its own good and a talent for making its students want to drop out of its courses. That's why I started to get seriously into making short films.

I always had made little short films. Well not always, I mean I didn't film anything in the womb for pretty obvious reasons. No camera, see? No, look, when I say always, I'd make haunting little slips of things since my early teens with the two friends that I had back when I had any friends. And I'd edited them as best as I could without professional equipment. Cared for them, kept them, learned from what didn't work so that by the time I was eighteen and joining the filmmaking society at University it really did feel like I'd been making the things for ever. And for many of the other students, who hadn't been spending their teenage years persuading their only friends to look enigmatic on their fifth take in a quiet car park, I may as well have. I was the expert. And didn't I feel it. Suddenly an oracle and top of the pile, getting Student Union funding to film the drama society pillocking about, filming protests in Trafalgar square and thinking I was filming history. I was, but so was everyone else. Filming promotional material for the Students' Union, stuff that actually played over the huge wall in the main hall on the open day. Tempting people to come to the University I couldn't be bothered with. Guess that was the time I realised that film really was lying to order

Not that I was as cynical as I'm making out now, at all. No, if anything, I was too wide-eyed about the possibilities of what I was getting myself into. A bit of early success seems to do that very well. I sent off some of my student films to little festivals up in Proper London and blow me if they didn't get shown and shortlisted for awards.

I was twenty by this point. Yes, I was probably insufferable. Who couldn't be? Look, I'm sure you can guess where I'm from, or rather where I'm not from. I'm not like lots of them out there, I'm not from an archetypal class or place. My folks, bless them, did such a lot in their lives and there was no medal or recognition or riches for them, just continued survival. I recently found some black and white photos in a tube roll buried in the box room of their place. I'd forgotten that Mum had been well into her photography when she'd been–well, when she'd have been my age then. Even younger, perhaps, seventeen or so. So sad, that adulthood fell on her and the time to do it vanished. It happened a lot then, as I now understand. I get that now.

And we didn't come from anywhere, so when my shabby little efforts got approval from some successful types – bingo!

I felt as if I was coming into my own, coming home. My home was, ah still is really, erm, an in-between town. Not London, really can't say I'm from there although it's what I say to anyone from outside of here. Not London at all but too far from anywhere else to be part of that, either. Mention its name and people think you're talking about the airport or the service station.

What I'm getting at is, we didn't feel like we were from anywhere or due for anything. I was a young woman (just getting used to calling myself that, never girl. I never want to be called a girl again, thanks) who was doing these things, and getting recognition, of a kind, but I had no sense of given purpose or entitlement to what seemed to be on the menu. I'd come from nowhere and it looked like I could actually end up somewhere. It felt like something was rising up from beneath me and carrying me along with it.

Early in my third year an invitation came. An invitation as opposed to an application I'd filled out. It came to me through the filmmaking society, and it was from a production company. I knew them. Modish stuff, selfconsciously edgy films all made for very little and starring TV actors presumably having a blast away from their recurring incomes, playing against type as odd outsiders and doing something the tea time audiences would balk at seeing their favourite soap stars in.

Neverleless, this company had a definite cachet. Grunge was still in the air, having taken a few years to permeate in the cultural petri dish from music to film and even theatre. Theatre! Hah! It was catching on. Never underestimate the desire for middle-class audiences to hear about what a load of shit they are, eh?

Anyway, they'd seen some of my little films and liked them enough to invite me to create something for a short festival one of their head bods was curating in some East London arts centre. I had six months to get something together, basic rules on what to include, and -most improbable of all, an allocated amount of money to actually make sure it happened.

For me. An invitation directed to me, alone, as a director. I put the note down and didn't look at it for a day or two in case when I did I found that I'd imagined what I'd read entirely and it was actually addressed to the other types in the society who only wanted to make little knock-offs of whatever gangster-phallic-wish-fulfilment was passing through the multiplexes at the time. Or again, if I read it properly or slowly would I find that they'd sent it to me but because they thought I was the most talentless cunt they'd ever had the displeasure of seeing and they wanted to take the opportunity of specifically telling me that I should never get behind a camera again? Hey, could have been, right?

No. I read it again, several times over, read it to my housemates, the twerpy boyfriend, over the phone to my parents. They did indeed want me and were paying for me.

Now, as all this was happening a the start of my third year I should really have been focused on getting to the academic finishing line and justifying the course I'd taken; the grant I was living on (one of the last to get them, lucky me) and the grudging effort I'd put into the last two years. But after two years on working very hard on pretty much everything apart from the thing I was supposed to be doing, breaking this habit was hardly going to make up for the inertia that had descended on that front. Would it? Well, maybe it would have.

But I was being helped up another staircase entirely.

I had the script, the crew, the location sorted in weeks. Came so easily, filtering a remembered short story or dream (can't remember which, didn't stop to question where) from adolescence into a scenario that I could shoot around our concrete nutsack of a campus in the early mornings. It looked like a culmination of all my little films, I swear I never intended to put a stamp on them, like they were my thing, like I was dictating how they'd turn out. And I was never intent on playing to an audience, even though right then I knew I had, I had some kind of fan out there, paying me a wage to come up with something. A benefactor. I understand that it's a Dickensian conceit. But I couldn't tell you more as I hadn't read any Dickens back then and I'm too busy talking to you to do so at the moment. I hope this makes you feel special.

Anyway, look, it all felt so easy. I was asked to do it, came up with it, shot it without too much incident, which in London at an odd time of the day is quite something. Ok, a boom was mangled by a horny Alsatian and we were chased away from trying an exterior shot by a janitor who had too many silver teeth not to be taken seriously. All fun and games, and no-one got hurt apart from the boom and the dog's sexual pride. I even delivered it under budget, and realised that they hadn't asked for the return of any unspent funding. Which in a way, there wasn't. As soon as I realised what was left over the twerp and I disappeared for a weekend in Glasgow which I still can't really remember.

A word on the twerp. I'm hardly speaking from a position of maturity, but looking back at the little parade of Russian dolls that popped into my life with every year or so on from my GSCEs, I see a trend of increased confidence bringing me just the type of twerp I'd desired whilst being with the previous one. Didn't realise that was happening. And increased confidence and success gives you the twerp you desire, which is frequently the twerp you deserve. Sadly, for this one, I was already having feelings that one of us had another new partner waiting around the corner. And in my case, my desire was taken up with something else entirely.

Oh and the balance I had to take in faking responsibility whilst on the phone to my dear old folks was worth recognition in itself. Takes real creativity to invent course modules that don't exist, purely because you have no idea what you are supposed to be doing. God, lying takes a concerted effort, doesn't it? But hey, it's a form of creativity and I guess one begats another.

Maybe they knew. I was as much of a beginner at lying as I was at being an adult. I detected no sense of them knowing I was bigging up my enthusiasm for what I was supposed to be doing, but I'm sure I was as transparent as a kid would've been. Maybe that's what I was at the time, eh?

Either way, near to the end of that year I found myself in a grotty little cinema somewhere in Dalston, ready to see my little work up on its big screen, along with a few others, and to meet some of the names I'd stared at through increasingly smudgy correspondence.

As the cinema was right on the other side of London I'd had to sack off one of my final seminars. I hadn't even asked my flatmate to crib some notes about it for me or say that I was ill. I think both parties were so used to the situation that it wasn't worth my mentioning it.

I'd gone alone. The twerpy boyfriend had tried, but I wasn't having it. I couldn't share the experience through someone else's eyes, this had to be me, experiencing the whole thing for myself, ready to imprint everything as a memory for later –the first night I saw the work on a cinema screen, the first time I met real-life production people, the first time I –oh god, inner yuck –made an impression. And how, exactly, was I going to do that? Was I supposed to press gang every bod I saw, or just sit in a corner and let my directorial talent magnetise all the important people over to me?

In the end I didn't have time to think of these things. The underground was delayed in several directions and I ended up having to run to the cinema from some overground station, sweating into my hoodie and DMs, looking nowhere near as cool and dignified as I wanted to. Not looking cool and dignified at all. The reception in the foyer was already full and I didn't have to introduce myself, a warm bottle of beer was pressed into my hands by a pained looking usher. People were already filing in to the theatre. Most were around my age, student types giddy to be invited and laughing. I managed to notice that no-one else seemed to be alone. Others must have brought their plus ones. What the hell had I been thinking? I'd been selfish at the first opportunity, denying my bland beau a chance to come along, and now here I was looking like a saddo – and a sweaty one.

I scanned the crowd. In the chance I got I picked out some older types -by older, I mean the properly adult, ones that were working at something or other, something connected to film. These were the people I'd have to somehow gravitate to after the showings. I still had no idea how, and in the state I was in it seemed even harder.

There were nine films being shown. Nine, of around fifteen minutes each. Two and a half hours to sit through, and no idea when I'd be up. My lower half felt heavy and the rest felt dizzy, light. What would these people think? Oh, my stuff had won little competitions but I'd only shown my stuff to people in other, anonymous rooms by this point. For all I knew I could have been selected as the winner by two people fast-forwarding the replay in an editing studio who were keen to finish the takeaway in front of them.

No-one knew me. Dammit, I'm sure no-one knew each other, either, although it didn't feel like it as I was sat there. Even if I could slip away anonymously at the end of the night I'd hear any disparagement and keep it with me, festering away and perhaps reminding me that maybe I was just pretentious and being a dilettante. These thoughts were spreading across my brain like spilt ink when I realised that we were a few minutes into the second film and I hadn't taken either in at all. I hadn't clapped in between, didn't realise one was over and another starting, hadn't heard any sounds –polite or otherwise –from the hundred or so people sat there. Hadn't even drank. I tried to snap back into it, to focus on what was being shown, but the image was fading in and out of focus, not helped by the sweat that was trickling down from my brow and probably gothing up my mascara. It was suddenly over and I found myself clapping-well, politely patting my bottle of beer – for something I hadn't taken in at all.

Then I was on. Well, the film was, but I was the film and the film was me, as I'm sure you can gather. I looked through my fingers, but they were prised so far apart that I could see everything. My boots were tucked back at a right angle underneath the chair. Whoever was sat next to me – I could see them reacting, they were smiling askance at me from what I could make out in my peripheral vision, they could see that I was poleaxed by actually seeing it. Apart from the ambient sounds of the film, I was trying to pick up anything, any murmur or mutter that could signify a reaction. All was quiet. It seemed – I'm not colouring this in after the fact, but it seemed like a good silence.

Oh fuck it, there's no way of describing this without sounding like an achingly pretentious arty type, but you know there are good silences, and bad silences, and we all recognise them, even if you don't think you do. Alright, I'll explain. The year before I'd gone to see a student theatre production at my university. Which is always a bad idea. Anyway. It was something set in Australia in the 19th century when the European types were colonising it up, or whenever they colonised it up, 1920s? I don't know, I never read up on it properly. Anyway, as is the way with these things, one (and I think it was only one) role was of a native person. An aboriginal, y'know. Well, despite trying to audition everyone they could, the lot putting it on couldn't find any actors who were anything other than white as snow. So, rather than cutting the part (talk about being erased from history) they decided that this girl would, uh, 'convey' the fact that she was a native type rather than trying any ill-advised characteristics. The night I saw it the actor in question had other ideas, and a theatre of people who were only seeing the thing out of politeness were jolted out of their boredom by a half-dressed, unmistakably Surbiton girl hopping onto the stage covered in what seemed to be crudely applied Nutella, speaking in some strangled accent that sounded like something off the moon.

That. That, my friend, was a bad silence. A collective disbelief, inhalation of air, followed by a stillness around the point of focus where for them it must sound and look like everything else has been frozen. And that's because it has. The play finished quite soon after that, due to the fallout. I think she left university soon after that night, actually. Either killed herself or went to work for a charity somewhere far away and hot.

Anyway, yes, a good silence is a different energy, a different atmosphere entirely. Its intent, but not in anticipation of release. Totally receptive. Rare, because few is the time when an audience is collectively really focused on something, taking it in like that. I could tell, I swear. No conversations starting up, no movement out of the side of my eye- the smiler next to me was looking straight ahead, not even taking it in my increasingly shaky state. Then it was over. I gulped at the stale farty old cinema air. Silence, again. I was waiting for a guffaw or heckle that would prove my hopes wrong, a little inner voice had already warned me that I was hoping too much and mistaken, they'd actually hated it. A nanosecond after the credit screen disappeared the applause started. It carried on into the credits for the next one. The woman next to me cupped her hand over her mouth –

'They really liked that, then,'

I made to mumble but nothing came out.

What were the rest of the films like? Oh, fuck knows. Expect me to remember? All I remember is relief. The films were...well, I wasn't getting instantly arrogant but I didn't remember much as each of them swam in front of me for a few minutes and then vanished. I remember some audience laughs, ripples of things that went around as a collective burble. I joined in, knowing that if I'd seen any of them on my own Id've probably stayed silent. Or not bothered watching at all.

It was soon done. I'd been decompressing for the remainder of the run, and suddenly realised that I couldn't remember what happened next. My beer was empty. No-one was moving, and I wasn't going to move on my own.

One of the houselights came on, and two figures strode on to the stage, into its beam. One was bearded and big mouthed, with shiny teeth that were visible from my row. The other was wearing a cap indoors –the unmistakable mark of a bald director. I guessed that the giant-mouthed beard was the producer.

The beard spoke. We were thanked, all thanked repeatedly and told how proud we should be of ourselves, and that they were glad to have asked us to contribute. He said that as a young filmmaker at our stage of career (career! Great, so it's going to happen? We've been anointed?) he would have been really glad to have had such an opportunity to show his work, and have a small amount of help to do so (no shit – I was glad that I had been able to make something to commission and not have to take the production costs out of my food budget). We were all emerging artists in our own right who'd come onto their radar because our previous work had stood out, so he was hoping to be able to speak to us afterward and see how things were going and what our plans were.

The director then stepped forward to add to the platitudes but his microphone wasn't working so for a minute or so we watched a faceless, capped face flap its lips at us. No-one was brave enough to point out that we couldn't hear. Too beholden to the situation to point out that something wasn't working, or too worried about giving a bad impression, perhaps? I'm sure everyone was along with my thinking on that front.

The lights came up full, and we did what cinema audiences rarely did, and looked around at each other, properly taking the rest of us in. All right, we were mostly young, mostly male and very noticeably pallid (hopefully from spending daylight in editing suites rather than scurvy). As I'd guessed. Scant oestrogen. Half of me swelled with pride – even in this select lot, I'm not like the others! Whilst the other half juddered – even here in my natural habitat I'm in essence a freak, and soon to be found out.

No, look, I swear – I remember the looks coming back at me from the beady little wank-worn eyes around the room. As soon as they registered me the look was slightly taken aback, then exited, then strangely threatened, all within and instant. Girl! I knew they'd register me as that, rather than woman. Growing up with boys, you get to know their though processes better than they do. After that I'm sure they'd be running through the credits of the parade of shorts we'd just seen and wondering if I was the one female director on the list.

Looking at the numbers in the room, I was now acutely aware that no-one else could have come on their own, most must have more than a plus one along, there were groups that must have been the core of the crews. Sharing in their little victory. Oh hell! Why had I been so self-absorbed. Had I even asked the poor people who helped with mine? I couldn't remember. Laura the loner, unconsciously playing the auteur and now looking quite the friendless fool.

We were being ushered out, so the stare-off didn't last long. Given my friendless state and engendered isolation, I wanted to duck out for fresh air, but remembered that I was in Dalston and there wasn't any, so allowed myself to be shuffled on.

We were in an adjacent bar, which looked nice but had a sticky floor – even though the place was just filling up the sucking and slapping sound of scuffed twentysomething converse trainers moving around the place was striking. The place must have been recently cleaned as I could smell bleach – not exactly a party smell, although I wasn't sure if this was exactly a party. The room was a narrow oblong with a little shitty cocktail bar at the far end, where the two men from the stage were already waiting, sipping from bottles of beer that looked expensive enough for me to not recognise it. After all this time of waiting and looking forward to the meeting, to the recognition – all I wanted to do was bottle it and run, but I was already on display and the way out was already blocked by the rest of the gaggle of youth, who seemed to have no trepidation. Of course –they were young men heading to free beer and and approval. Nothing was going to stop them. I allowed myself to be buffeted away to the side of the room, where I found a footing underneath a framed photo of Groucho Marx, Chaplin, one of them.

Looking down to the bar, I could see that the hosts were already in conversation with some of the more confident attendees, who were nodding and putting so much effort into looking attentive that they must have been missing some of their hosts' conversation. I overheard nuggets of others' conversations – halting, introductory, cursory. No-one was really conversing, they were marking time until the one conversation they wanted to have, and – of course – had been mentally preparing themselves for. I hadn't given any thought to this. Really. Oh, I'd half-dreamed of discussing the actual work over a desk with one of the company in some office somewhere after it had been shown, but an office is not a sticky bar, and I hadn't imagined around a hundred other competitors for time swaying around and stepping on my shoes.

I've never been the kind to actually big themselves up in person. I don't believe anyone who's grown up in a semi-detached house in a shunned town can. That's the preserve of people who either come from nothing and have no option but to blast themselves into opportunity, or were born into so much opportunity that they don't realise it and don't realise they're hollering over other people. If you were brought up in the squishy grey middle, like me, there's no extremity and no impetus to raise your voice over another's. Ok, maybe I'm reading myself into the overall situation, but isn't that the way of the artist? Or maybe I'm not enough of a dickhead. I can't be the only one who's made stuff, dedicated so much time and effort and sacrificed other acres of opportunity, and then been aghast at the fact that I had to explain myself in public, and stand up in front of strangers and hype not only the work and why they should watch it, but who I was and why I should be given money to make more and what I'd be doing next if I was given that. What's the connection between the person who makes the work and the one who has to go out parping a horn to draw up attention for it? Still don't get that.

Now, I wasn't exactly thinking this to the letter as I was buffeted toward the two important but glib looking men at the bar, but there was certainly a putative version unfurling in my mind. Who the fuck were these people, really, and why the fuck was I going to have to not just talk to them but give some kind of impression, something that would lead to more meetings, something quite outside the work that had just been shown and should have been doing all the talking for me, if talking outside of the thing was ever needed?

There's no inherent connection between the maker and the hyper, and there certainly wasn't one in the young woman, girl, who was drifting toward the bar at that point in time. The film was certainly going to have to speak for itself. Whether it wanted to or not.

The throng was so squashed in the little oblong room that it would have taken too concerted, too obvious an effort, to try and push my way through them to escape, and the movement meant that I couldn't stay still - I was being incrementally moved by the churn of sweaty young men, none of whom I chose to engage with. I had nothing to say to them, and they knew they didn't have anything to say to me, they hadn't had anything to say to each other either, from what I'd been able to hear. Oh, I'm sure I looked aloof or arrogant rather than seized up and shy to the situation. It's been said over the intervening years, that's how I come across. Fine, in many of the situations I've found myself in silence and non-engagement have been the better option. Plus, sometimes it's actually hard to engage with dickheads. And sometimes you'll only find out how much of a dickhead a person is by interacting with them, so play it safe and keep yourself quiet, is my advice to you and you can pass that on to humanity as a whole.

A supremely tanned waitress had just handed me a glass of lukewarm white wine, which was literally unasked for, when that booming voice vocalised in my direction-

-It's Laura! Now, Laura, come over, we want to congratulate you!'

I allowed the crowd to move me forward, and felt an imagined spotlight picking me out of the sweaty crowd. I'm sure I was blinking in response. No getting out of this now. I was kind of glad that I hadn't even unconsciously prepared anything as it would have been out of the window as soon as I opened my mush, anyway.

-That's a really good film. Very distinctive, very you –it's connected to your other work. We're all fans, here. Hero! This is David Quest-

-Good ev -

-We're very glad to meet you. How did you find seeing your work up there?

Had he just called me a hero?

-So I gadda that you're still at University?

-Yes – well, not tonight.

-No, obviously.

I still don't know why the hell I said that. I wasn't trying to be witty. Thankfully.

-What will you do after? Ten-pin?

-Sorry?

-Ten-pin?

-Uh, yes. Well I don't know.

The reverberating noise of the non-conversations around us were making some of the producer's booming hard to follow.

-We always need rubbers.

I didn't know how to respond to that. I was still trying to establish what had been said, and if it was what it sounded like, when something new came along. Funny how when you look back over the recent past you can see yourself passing by the door that you'll eventually walk through.

-Well, David and I have discussed this. I don't want to pasturise you, but it's worth letting you know that we'd like to wok with you in some cat bassand tea. OK. Let's see what comes through the pipeline. Do you have an Asian yet?

-Do I have an Asian?

-Yes, have you been approaching people? It's worth you pudding your elf out hair.

Now the director, who had been mostly murmuring assent to the words that were booming in and out of audibility, nodded and interjected-

-We'll see if we can help, but –

Here he cupped his hand to the side of his face, making a sound tunnel with his still tightly affixed cap

-We'll be happy to help out if nothing's happened yet. But think about what we've been saying-

I was thinking a lot about what they'd been saying, and trying to make sense of it

-And give us a call when you're ready. Here's our card. Keep it safe and give us a call. Do you have one?

-A phone?

-No, a card.

-Well, no, I don't really have a production company yet. I'm still studying.

-Well, you've got a good team already, might be worth keeping them close in case they get snapped up by someone else.

By whom, I wondered? None of the other students who had helped me on the shoot had expressed any hunger to go into film. In fact, they seemed mildly embarrassed to be part of it. At least, they were when we were being pursued by dogs down dodgy London streets. Given the benefit of a few years' hindsight, I'm inclined to agree with them after the fact.

-Oh, well fuck the team, eh?

Why the hell did I say that?

-Sorry?

-Ah, I said, up the team! Couldn't have done it without them. I'll let them know that you said they were good.

Like they'd give a fuck. Like I'd remember to tell them in the first place.

The beard was now booming again.

Very nice of you to think of 'em, that's a good collaborative spirit. Keep that card safe, but here – put your number on this. Stand out stuff.

I used the biro he handed to write my flat's phone number. This was just before the rise of the mobile, so giving out numbers frequently resulted in confused housemates taking calls from strangers whilst you were in the shower or out drinking.

As happened. Yes, once I was back on the train and processing what was said I realised that I'd been given a definite offer. An offer of work in film. It was, trust me, euphoric. But had they said the same to all the other types there? I couldn't tell. I certainly didn't see any other cards being handed out. I hadn't seen anyone reeling away with the kind of smug expression that would signify the offer of work, and being young men they were probably far more used to decoding conversations in noisy bars than I was.

I still didn't know what the hell the beard had meant by needing rubbers with regularity and was flipping that over in my mind as the stations went by. Was this some sexual reference? Surely not? Why would a shoot need a constant stream of prophylactics, unless it was a strangely abstemious porn production? And if that was the case, what would my role in that be? Procurer? Rubber-wrangler? Maybe it was. Maybe they used young people desperate for experience and wages to roll on the rubbers to the cock of the day?

By the time I was leaving the city, I was trying to suppress that scenario and instead understand why he'd wanted me to have an Asian. Was this about who I was going out with? Was this the chic thing – especially if you were a woman? In my quivering, paranoid state I'd sometimes wondered if the industry I was trying to headbutt myself into was the stew of perversity that rumour, cliché and outright documentation pointed to. Had I the knowledge then, I would have realised that I was, essentially, right. But in all the wrong directions.

I didn't have any answers to these scary thoughts, and they weren't going to resolve themselves without some outside input. For the present, I tried to quell them and focus on what seemed – really seemed, oh bless my prepared-for-disappointment-all-my-suburban-little-life-self; to be a moment of real triumph.

I hadn't even allowed myself to think of a job offer being whacked around my chops like that. You know the deal, it's the same for everyone. Even if you don't realise it. Before you go into some kind of meeting, something that you know is about to happen, like a date, a drink or a meeting with your boss: your mind is always imagining it for you, coming up with variations about what can happen. Depending on the kind of brain you've been developing all your life, it could be coming up with the best or worst-case-scenario. If it's a date, probably the former, guess it's what we'd all want. If it's the meeting with your boss it's probably imagining what could happen in the worse-case-scenario; as a safety precaution, you're imagining how you're going to react to what could be happening soon.

It's like a subconscious fail-safe, I'd guess. Now, in my case my excited old brain was pushing a few possibilities at me on the way in, and these were only becoming apparent as I was making my way back, here's a few-

You were invited by accident!

Your film is dogshit compared to everyone elses' and you will be roundly mocked by absolutely everyone and that absolutely includes the professionals who will specifically tell you that you aren't cut out for this and when everyone has finished laughing can you please leave AS SOON AS POSSIBLE,

Everyone loves the film and the professionals want to speak to you but as soon as you try you shit yourself,

It's actually a prank cooked up by the debating society who are still really pissy about you using the lecture theatre when they thought they'd booked it but they hadn't and when you pointed this out you made their president cry he was so embarrassed,

-(slightly less likely this but it did occur to me more than once, seemed like the thing they'd do)

So when I was there, failing to hear most of the important conversation, something in me was still anticipating one of the above scenarios happening, whilst the rest of my brain was tempering my excitement by refusing to believe in the reality of what seemed to be suggested. It continued to do so until I was on that grotty late night tube, only then with the tinnitus blocking out the sound of the tube drinkers did I allow myself to totally believe what had been said.

Everyone else I told believed me instantly, all right. Well, they said they did, even if they didn't. The current drip was delighted for me when I got home, and offered to celebrate in a way that he was used to me declining.

Although to be fair, this time I really was tired and really not in the mood.

Throughout the rest of my time at University the ladder to a different, worthwhile future was at the periphery of my vision. Constantly. In every lecture I was now forcing myself to attend. Leading up away from my damp room every time I was trying to eke out a piece of semi-improvised history to essay length. At my graduation (yeah, just squeaked a 2:2) whilst I sweated in a dark robe off Gower Street, wondering if my poor folks were going to kiss me or cry, those long stairs were leading right up from behind the podium where the vice-chancellor was giving what I can only imagine is the usual peroration speech for undergraduates, about the future, importance of what we've done and will do, yadda yadda. I wonder if Vice Chancellors have standard texts that they share with each other, like the standard essay answers students around the world share now and try to get away with? Either way, they'd probably be safe to do so as the graduates – sorry, graduands, are never listening, they're thinking Oh shit it's all over and what the fuck do I do now and the more perceptive may wonder throughout what the fuck was all that for? Well. I'm not universal, I can't vouch for future generations. But I keep my ear to the ground.

Then, in that hall, I was thinking something different. I was thinking why haven't I contacted them yet?

It had been four months. I'd finished University. Dispensed with the drip. He was easy to jettison, would have been easier if he'd read the runes correctly. I was divesting myself of encumbrances, and they were two. I'd even, in a panic at the thought of having to move back to my folks, accepted an offer from a school friend to live with her and some others in a place at the very end of the central line with cheapo rent. Dammit, I'd even send my c.v off to some reputable employment agencies who were getting me interviews in adequate but indescribably boring office jobs.

All the above things were possible for lower-middle-class suburban types to do in London back then. I know, what a mad fantasy. I swapped one end of London for another. Having grown up in a place where no-one recognised as from anywhere, I now started my adult life (don't laugh) in a part of London that no-one from the rest of London thought was part of it. We were in a house off a broadway of shops, with the tube station by it, but beyond that were fields. Manky fields, but you couldn't argue with the field-ness of them.

I had started to get to bed at vaguely decent times. I dressed acceptably. All had changed. I felt like part of the grown-up world, putatively. Why had I...

...why had I bottled it?

I knew why, really. Scared. Shit scared. Because, my friend, the creative mind (as yours no doubt is) is inclined to both talent and neurosis, and even compliments and the offer of coming on board to joining the exalted club can result in not joy, arrogance, but outright fear.

If you don't believe that, come on, think, how many times have you found yourself in a good situation only to worry that you weren't worthy of it? That you would be found out? So it is with many of us who get the chance, and balk, freeze, because this could be the moment when we get found out as nothing. When they, and we, find out that everything we thought we'd brought up out of nowhere was nothing but a fluke, a blessing that stayed with us for a miracle time and then ran like the clappers when we needed it the most. Leaving us looking like the most hapless, talentless cunt imaginable.

Yes, I guess it was kind of cowardly. I was being dishonest with myself, and even though all seemed well outwardly there was a churning within. It's an easy thing, to not be sure what you're supposed to be doing at that age, and easier still to not know the solution. But I did know. I wanted to be directing. I needed to me making films. And this wasn't an idle cloud of thought, I'd been doing it, I'd had a helping hand offered to me. But I had frozen at the point of everything being offered, and even though I don't think I consciously knew it at the time, the offer had scared me as much as it had excited. And so here I was now, taking the tube into town to stare at spreadsheets and flipcharts.

So, you see, I ran toward this life, then jumped back from it. But as you can tell, I've ended up here anyway. How?

They called me.

I'd been living off the broadway at the end of London for a few weeks. That day, I'd sacked off the temp job because it was a Friday and I couldn't be arsed. You could afford to do that kind of thing back then. I'd gone out to the Woolworth's shop to buy some much-needed cleaning items for our kitchen. We weren't students any more, but student habits were dying hard.

My housemate had left the note by the phone (no answerphone for us), and the wobbly scrawl showed that she had written whilst holding the 'phone.

'Loud man called Hero called. Asked for you about coming to work with them.

Alice, 2pm'

Jesus! How?

I'd passed him my flat's phone number but not this one. He must have called that place and got through to Alice's old friend who remembered that I'd moved in with her, and still had her number. And he had pursued. By a tiny thread, my chance had survived and re-iterated itself. I was taken aback mostly by that, but also by the fact that he was called Hero. Aside from the inherent dickishness of that, I'd thought he had been using it as a kind of catchphrase or salutation when he'd been talking. After all, it seems to make more sense used in that way as opposed to being a name to be saddled with. God! How can you not help but live down to a name like Hero? And how can parents –or a parent – shove their baby off into life saddled with that. Unless they're convinced their spawn will live up to such an arrogant moniker. Well, we know now...

Of course I phoned back.

'Ah, Laura-'

(This was back when people, even him, could remember my name)

-thanks for phoning back. I hadn't realised you'd moved, but there's a position open in a new shoot that's starting this week. Not pencilled in, actually shooting. In Wales. Someone's dropped out. Can you start tomorrow?'

You can tell that with the staccato rhythm of these sentences, coupled with the natural volume of this man's voice, I had little opportunity of getting a word in, and by the time the question was asked I couldn't respond. Like any half-smart person in that context, I wanted more time, but as was made clear to me, that was not in supply. One of the few lessons I've learned over a few years in this industry, there – whatever is going on, there's never enough time. Like, look where we are now.

Anyway, I said yes. Sometimes you've got to take the risky option, I remember rationalising to myself. The temp job would have to remain sacked off for the foreseeable. The bags were soon packed, and within two days I was second assistant director on a short film being shot on the Gower peninsula between bouts of biblical drizzle. Note the job title. I didn't note it beforehand, as no-one had mentioned it to me. Second assistant director as opposed to first assistant director, or indeed assistant director. So there was directing involved, for sure, but directing stuff that the director or assistant director or first assistant director couldn't or wouldn't do. Thinking back, this frequently meant making sure that the actors were on the right scene, the extras weren't looking in the camera (and getting rid of those that were) and making sure that the venue for the next few days' shoot was ready and free.

So it was dogsbody stuff, but not the kind of stuff I'm doing now. Look, at the time I was happy to be paid to work on something – anything – in film and I felt like at that point I could only go up. Ha ha, you're thinking, I know. That wasn't just naivety. I was promised more.

This was just the apprenticeship. That was how it was couched. This was just a traineeship for running a shoot myself, they had an opening that would allow me to pick up what I needed to keep a set running myself. How had this position opened? Had someone quit? I didn't ask. I trained myself not to, and then grew used to not doing so.

Really, for the first year or two of doing this kind of thing, I was too high on the fact that I was working regularly on a set to see that after a few shoots, the route I was being funnelled into, deliberately or not, wasn't even remotely leading to the destination promised. What can I say, being busy can keep you from seeing what you're really doing.

And so it went. Different shoots, different places, but they kept me on. A few across the year, of different lengths, but enough to pay my share in the little place on the edge of London, where I'd return and have to immediately start to look for temp work, across a range of increasingly irked agencies. Sometimes, you see, the call would come in and I'd have to leave one of their jobs with little notice. Well, that happened a few times and my lack of notice started to be noticed. So the more I hooked along with one potential, promised future, the more I undercut my chances with another. The latter being the one that would have provided me with more stability and a shot at having a normal life. But, ah, I was too young to be thinking of those things. Tell me, is that the natural state of youth? Thinking of and running after the very things you shouldn't?

Anyway. What I should have been doing, I didn't, and I kept on this path, the one that's brought me to this permanently out-of-sorts seaside town, working on a film that, look, I really don't know if it will get finished for the first thing, let alone seen by anyone other than the editor if it does. And yes, mostly making tea and carrying around costumes.

I didn't see it coming until it was too late. You're doing less of camera work on one shoot, then you do the same thing on another, another two, then the next time they say they have less of it to do but this needs to be done as someone's dropped out and there's no other option but for you to fill that as it needs doing, and-

-and then you're just doing the dogwork and you have to think hard to remember when you were behind a camera, in any context. But you're stuck in this course because the last time you were back and looking for other stuff to pay the rent in London (which is whirling up, year by year, incidentally) they were offering you even more dogshit work for even less than you'd get on a shoot.

So you take it, and wonder when. When you'd even get the time or wherewithal to shoot a little short on your own, how; where's the money, where's the crew, the help, when was the last time you saw any of your old friends from University, because-

-without looking, or feeling the water rise around you, that's the amount of time gone, it's years now and they're 'old friends' and you don't really have new ones. Just the occasional regular colleague and they 'aint really friends in the old sense and you can't remember the last time you saw any of the old friends and you don't know when you or they would get the time. Let's be bloody brutal here you're a bit worried in the stomach that maybe it's been too long and if you do meet them you'll be staring over at them and them back at you, both parties wondering if it just isn't the same and whether it's worth seeing each other again.

It goes in, this treadmill. Still, at least I don't have much stress as such in my private life. Because there isn't any private life to speak of. Just sweaty, worried nights alone.

Still, it's showbiz, eh. The folks tell their friends and the rest of the family all they need to know, oh yes, she's still working on the films, yes she's on one now, that's why she hasn't been able to come over to visit, long hours but she's happy. That's even when I'm not working on one, of course.

Or is that what I tell them myself? And maybe they choose to believe it, maybe they're keeping a faith in something else coming up, even if I've lost it?

Dunno. We never choose to broach these things, do we? Big stuff. Oh fuck, listen to me, I'm so tired I've got a bit morbid. I guess self-examination can do that to you. Or to one, as some of the crew would say. Hero. Zephiah.

So it's been a trying few years, inwardly. I knew, inwardly, that I'd hit the skids when I was commandeered to fumigate the set and costumes on a music promo when it transpired that one of the band had caught scabies and tried to keep it quiet from everyone. We knew something was up when he couldn't complete some rudimentary dance steps because he wouldn't stop scratching himself around his nuts. Hey, I thought it was just that his jeans were too tight. Which they were anyway, let's be honest.

I'd hoped to have been directing things of my own, and there I was exterminating microscopic lice. One of those unpleasant situations that just comes up. Unpleasant situations have had a habit of doing that, with increasing frequency. It's a matter of chaos and trust, I think. You trust those in power that they'll have your back, with the underlying knowledge that in this daft game your time will be mostly taken up with boredom and repetition, spiked by the occasional explosion of chaos. In those moments you have to believe that if there's genuine danger within that, someone will be able to make sure that you're safe from harm.

You have to believe that. Doesn't mean that it's true.

Take now, with this thing. By 'thing', I'm talking about the film, and Dermot. We've already had him knock out a priest, so there's been one definite victim, and that seems to be being hushed up and suffocated off stage. They'd be fucked if any media were actually interested in this film or who was making it. Maybe. But there's something beyond the pale with the guy even bearing the priest-punching in mind. No-one can read him and I'm convinced he can't read himself, either. There's a lifetime of waywardness working with us and I think we've all crossed paths when he has either stopped giving a fuck or is just about to do so. But, but look, because he's working well – on screen – there's been no hint of firing him or at least restraining him with something so there's no chance of a repeat outburst.

Maybe it's because we don't have the budget. Maybe it's because we don't have the time.

I mean, I'm used to working with lunatics and people at the end of a tiny tether. I've been working with actors and film-makers for years. I've dealt with truculence, basic incompetence, moon-units and would-be-divas, but they didn't faze me like this one. I grew up with an antsy dog so I knew how to deal with them all, the methods are similar. Make them calm down, distract them, threaten and shout to show who's boss if needed. Pain in the arse, but it's always worked.

But I never felt in any physical danger from any of that lot. This is different, and I know that the rest of the crew have been thinking the same, more and more, it's a feeling of unease that's permeating the set now. Now it's too late to do anything about it. And let me tell you (god, I'm starting to sound like some old lady veteran of film shoots) the more this builds up around everyone, the more chance there is of other types of weird behaviour busting out of someone else. Like when someone turns up drunk somewhere when they're supposed to be sober, but it's one of the sober people who end up slurring their words and behaving weirdly. People are getting jittery already, I heard one of the cameramen barking at someone to get out of the honeywagon today, when he'd seen that the other bloke had only just gone in. Must have been barely mid-dump.

Why's he here, that's the question. Rule of thumb – no matter who you are in the biz, when you're looking for work you have to be acutely conscious that there's a plethora of people fitting your description and talent right behind your shoulder. This should be especially acute whilst working, as you have to acknowledge the brutal truth that if you kick off (or, more chillingly, if the powers that be decide that it just isn't working out with you), then one of those people will be turning up on set shortly after you have left, if not before. Can you see why there's an underlying jitteriness permeating every social strata on these sets? And can you see why I've kept my little paws in the game, for finding that I've been replaced if I leave it for a while?

There's lots of leathery character actors out there. Lots who are sane, nonviolent and (improbable as it may sound to you) sober. This geezer in question is none of the above, and hasn't been since my folks were in school. It's his reputation, it's overshadowed his actual work for decades. Apparently it has, in fact, been the drain down which his career has been flowing since I was in nappies. And yet the record shows that he's done a couple of films, plays, in a decade or so. Some casting directors must be far more lenient than I'd thought, or plain gullible in the face of tales of sobriety. Again, my director of photography friend let slip that bad things happened to these productions. And I don't just mean that apparently they were shite and made no money.

No, our undead friend here has fans close by.

It's a factor related to the kinds of people who normally find themselves making films once they hit full adulthood. Let's think back to that screening in Dalston. Yes, the young men. Young movie-mad nerds who find themselves in a position to be able to make their own and want to use as many of the toys in the box they've found themselves in possession of. The raw talent that is people, faces from films they watched too many times on their worn out VHSs across their adolescence and dark-roomed early youth. Guess these people, be they actors or Directors Of Photography or editors could be seen as lucky amulets, or maybe they want an experienced, elder head to work alongside their tyro selves.

Dermot had, whilst his career was already in early skid phase, made some abominable shockers with some cheapo English film companies. They have stuck in the collective nerd brain quite well, if not mine, and this is what years later made him Hero and David's first and seemingly only choice for this role, that of a curmudgeon growing to love life. Yes, the gist of the role really is that trite, I'm afraid. I've never seen the films in question, by the way, but they don't strike me as work that a previously feted film star would jump up and be proud of.

Either way, I heard word that despite the casting director's seasoned warnings about old Dermot and his habits, she was told by Hero and David that he'd be perfect for the part and despite the fact that his agent hadn't spoken to him for several years and didn't know where he lived, or what state he was in, alright wasn't even 100% sure that he was still alive; he'd be perfect for the part.

And, from what I've seen, from the footage we have in the can, he is perfect for the role. It's just the rest of the shoot, the rest of this flotilla of people, that I wish they'd thought of. Perhaps we're ultimately expendable next to the lead. But I can't help but think of the legion of wintry, craggy types out there who could do just as well surely, who wouldn't be found wrestling Labradors outside a betting shop mid-morning when they're needed on set. Who don't howl at an absent moon every once in a while.

It's getting stranger every day, and it's permeating everything, the growing sense of refracted madness. He has his little tent that he stays in in between takes. This is fitted with a small heater. We have to do this because in a coastal town insurance simply won't let us have someone of Dermot's age stood around for any amount of time. Given the hissed muttering and the staring at things that aren't there that he usually does when he's round people, that should be fine. When he's away there's a marked decrease of tension. But it's like a six-foot chrysalis, at the periphery of our collective vision, dark and emitting odd barks and recriminations. People fight to avoid having to be the one to bring him out of there. And guess who the loser is, increasingly.

Still, I've probably ended up doing so because I'm brave enough to actually do it, apart from the fact that very few around – or left – have a lower status than me here. I've gotten off lightly, so far. The first waves of fear went round after what happened to the 1st AD.

It was three days in and we were shooting in a patch of allotments on one of the town's hills. The location had been scouted and selected as it has a view over the town and the bay that looks amazing when the light hits it. All we needed were a few pick-ups of his character looking up from his marrows or prunes (or whatever they are, muddy veg) up over the camera to his departing daughter. A couple of words to mutter, almost under his breath, that would be synched in foley later. Not too taxing on the face of it, but then most shoots aren't. The main point was to get the man, the expression and the scenery behind, look, here he is in his coastal retreat, oh, the lovely countryside here to give us profit!

Problem one was the fact that the forecast lied , and the sun-kissed bay we were getting in shot was soon covered in gunmetal grey clouds. A sudden and persistent coastal wind also gave the impression that King Kong was constantly farting the allotment off its roots. Bucolic it wasn't.

Now, we crews are used to this kind of stuff, we were, under whatever tarpaulin we had and ready for when nature would stop it and allow us to do our job. It's miserable in a sense, but when all present have the intent and focus to get it done, no matter how soggy they are, it can make for the kind of day where if the shot does happen everyone knows that the job has been done and can collapse into bar and bed tired but happy.

So when the sun was coming through, we knew we had to work quickly. The wind had subsided from the earlier level but could still bring dark cover over soon. We were all ready.

But with no Dermot. The tent was perhaps ten meters behind the main set-up, and we knew he was there, as mutterings had been heard. David had sent a runner over twice, who had wilted back after receiving a barking from within. It was then, when all had been perfectly ready to go and clouds could already be seen on the far horizon, that David pulled down his cagoule hood, struck a manly pose-and told the 1st AD to go and get him out of the tent, no exception.

This was received grudgingly, at best, by the 1st AD, who wouldn't normally have to do such a task, but probably realised that we couldn't afford to go a day behind at this stage and more importantly he couldn't afford to say no to David.

All were watching him as he squelched up to the tarpaulin cylinder, with the clouds growing ominous behind it.

He'd barely opened the zip before the bottle hit him, plastic, thankfully, but spurting and foaming an unmistakably yellowy liquid. He was hit right in the face, and others instantly fled to escape the urinary radius.

After an aghast second or two I and some others were over to him, helping him to get steady. The 1st AD was silent, but not for long. The only voice I heard at that point was the 2nd AD –

'It's piss, alright.'

That was the first time something like that has happened so early on, and so drastic. And it's been the first time that I've really noticed that, if the people at the top want to keep you there, the consequences for any dreadful actions you sow will permeate throughout all the other people there, rather than you, the actual culprit.

I was the one that had to hose the 1st AD down, literally and metaphorically. He had no intention of quitting at that stage, as with most of us there he thought that Dermot would be either quitting or getting a boot up the backside.

That was the first resignation. We still haven't done the scene.

Resignation, mind. Not firing.

We had all decamped to our hotels despondently that night. Even the thrill of gossiping about such an outrage happening so soon into a shoot was overrun by the stark feeling that if something like this had happened when we were barely starting, a bad few weeks were naturally going to flow.

The next day compounded this, when we saw Dermot on the call sheet but no name next to the 1st AD. Blank. He'd resigned.

At the time I thought that, although well within his rights, it was a bit of an overreaction. Now, well, I'd say it was a blatant display of sanity.

Phil the camera filled me in when we were on a break.

-After he was washed and dried he marched straight up to their production office-

(this was in an ostentatious Winnebago, which had made its home in a reliably empty car park near the seafront)

-and gave it to them both barrels.

-As they were going to expect, right?

-As I'm sure they were expecting. He demanded an apology. Right there and then.

-From them?

-Yes, from them, for allowing it to happen, but also from Dermot for doing it.

-And?

-And they apologised, alright, but said they wouldn't be able to get Dermot in.

-He was what, off grid?

-He's always off grid, even when he's here.

-Right, but they weren't going to make an effort?

-No, they said they were sorry it happened, but they wouldn't be able to get him in there and they weren't sure they'd be able to get an apology from him without jeopardising the rest of the shoot.

-That's mental, surely they should have been telling him to go throw his piss anywhere he wanted but on a film set?

-So we would have thought. But nothing was forthcoming. So he told them to fuck off. That he'd fuck off. And tell the union.

-Which union is he in?

-I don't think he's in one. Well, he was asking what one I'm in the other day and I'm not in one, that's as far as it went between us.

-So we've lost our 1st AD and kept captain pisshands?

-Bang on. What was his name, again?

-Dom. Derek. Danny. I don't know, actually, I don't think we got to that stage.

-Ok. This is weird.

-Yes, I've never seen anything like this happen this early on, it's usually when people have got to know each other. And it isn't usually piss.

- Still, time for the 2nd AD to step up.

-Correct. I wonder if she engineered this?

-I think you're reading too much into the whole thing.

Thankfully that day and the next were scenes with Zephiah and some of the day players...Zephiah, oh yes. I'd better reintroduce the leading lady. She's the one who has been cast to rein in as much public interest as possible, although this film is, supposedly, an arty little two-hander, a character piece, really it'll be her face on all the posters. And I can understand why, she'll draw them in.

Young. I can say that now, I guess, she can't be older than 22 and as I mentioned that's younger than most of the crew and definitely younger than me. But with that youth,having had several years of being the lead across all the kinds of screen and stage stuff this country offers. Self-possessed, as I guess you'd have to be to survive that kind of landscape from your teens to your early twenties. No damage on the surface, at least, but even with my half-arsed academic background I do wonder what that can do to your interior.

What I mean is, when other nice middle-class types were waiting tables and going to disappointing raves and studying some bullshit at University, and gradually becoming a frog rather than a tadpole, there she was auditioning and being cast and working with a stream of constant strangers and seeing your face on billboards and TV Now and having no private face of your own, and-

-all the time whilst having to be something other than yourself, even though, god, at that time, do you know

who the departure point is? Do you really have a clue about who you are, really? Ok, perhaps I'm skimming pretentiousness here, but I was thinking that the other day. Watching her doing a page of dialogue on her own to an off-screen interlocutor, private in the make-believe whilst maybe fifty people huddled around away from her sight-line. Me, sat at the back, trying to not drop a tray of something. That level of self-possession is eerie. In one so young. Have I earned enough years to say that? Am I coming off like some ancient mariner at the age of twenty-eight?

Maybe that's how I feel. But yes, Zephiah, simultaneously porcelain and radiant, came to the production straight from a west end hit. An especially esteemed one, you know the kind. Short run in a tiny theatre, so tiny that people can't actually get tickets, they just read the reviews and think that it sounds very important and worthy, whilst the only people who see it go to say they've seen it and I'm sure spend most of it needing a piss and when it's over wonder if they have an opinion to tell their friends about afterward. Quality stuff.

So I was primed for a right prick, as you can imagine. But since starting those weeks ago, Zephiah has been calm, thoughtful, co-operative, on time.

No-one has a good word to say about her. Well, no-one has managed to form an opinion on her, at the least. Granted, there's a more distracting, disturbing show in town, which is in her favour. I wonder if she's deliberately reined in any potentially damaging impulses in order to make herself even more distinct to the rest of us?

Or is she aware of her being in a shitter of a shoot, and has withdrawn into herself for the duration? We haven't, I mean it's not too abnormal to, have the occasional drink with your star on one of these things; but she's been elusive. Sam the clapper wonders if she's preggers. Ronnie the spark's putting it about that she's spending her spare time with a county cricketer who lives in a mansion nearby. Camera Phil says she may just be a bit dull when she doesn't have a pre-set scenario to latch on to.

I dunno. But she's self-possessed for sure. They've had a few scenes together, Dermot and her, and no matter how erratic he's been I haven't seen a complaint from her.

Now, that's not normal. Lateness, smelling of booze, threatening the extras, any of this would normally result in a conscientious co-star raising some kind of flag with the powers that be. If not because of their own concerns, to make it known to the rest of the crew that they themselves do not approve of such actions. All have happened, with not a peep out of her, as far as reports go.

It's gone smoothly as far as getting the scenes canned goes, but no-one has ever seen a word said between them. She's probably just a wary as the rest of us. As most of us. I had word from make up that when they were getting her ready they'd asked how her previous day's shoot with Dermot had gone. She said-

Well, someone was in there, and they did the work, and kept their piss to themselves.

Which is as diplomatic as one can get about him, I guess. And as near as she's skirted to gossip, so many weeks in.

Dermot, for his own part, has eluded her. I was worried, given how the state of play, or balance of power, can sometimes work out in these situations.

And all the while our leaders, the producer and director that seemed joined at the hip to me now, have remained weirdly serene. Earlier today Hero actually spoke to me. Deliberately, and no-one else was around.

-Lana!

(told you he tends not to remember what my actual name is now. Out of habit, I guess. I didn't have the time or authority to correct him)

How's it been going?

Given that I was carrying a sewn-up hat for one of the day players and I'd been trying not to trip up in a spew of black cables out back of one of the caravans, hadn't slept for a day and was so desperate for the loo I thought I was about to shit myself really; I couldn't answer with anything but an exhausted grunt that was trying to be some kind of affirmative. See, told you I didn't have it in me to be a bullshitter.

Good! Glad you're enjoying it. Really appreciate what you've been doing, especially as things have been tight.

Tight or shite?

Look-we would like to take a moment to see you. Once we're wrapped for today, could you make the time to meet David and I? Not for too long, I know we've been up for a long time.

Like any person on a lower rung who gets a speech like that, I started to feel a deep unease which I tried to suppress. Unfortunately as I'd been up so long my reactions were starting to go skewhiff, and instead of saying Absolutely, I slurred-

-Delicious.

Hero's silence made me wonder if I had actually said it. I didn't want to ask him if I'd just said delicious in case I hadn't as that would make the little conversation collapse into a warren of weirdness that it had until then avoided.

He wasn't saying anything yet, although it had probably only been a second or so after I'd possibly said something. I wondered if I should go back to my original plan of saying absolutely, but realised that all my reserves of energy were now focussed on not soiling myself and anyway, in my state I might say delicious again.

-Great...once we wrap we'll decamp to the heated Winnebago. I'll drop you a line. Can't promise you it'll be delicious, but should be some interesting work.

Absolutely. I didn't say.

Well, I dunno know what you've been up to all day, but I'm glad to see you. I'm not sure what I've agreed to do or why, but I'm seriously bricking it.

I met them in the Winnebago. It was the first time I'd properly been in there instead of just dropping teas off, and the bloody thing is better than most of the hotel rooms we have. It has more room than the rooms, really, not that they stay in it or anything.

The DOP told me they were ready about half an hour after we wrapped. I'd been helping out Continuity, getting the costumes safely put away, so was near by.

I still didn't have a clue about why I'd been properly asked in, and had spent the last few hours trying to glean any reactions from the rest of the crew, any sign that they knew why I'd been singled out, any sly glint in their eye. None. All were too preoccupied with their own tasks, keeping their own heads above the mire. I was still shattered, although I'd caught at least three minutes' shut eye after the last tea run, slumped on a stool behind the honeywagon, still close enough to hear the alert if I was needed for something. Yes, a couple of minutes and the call was out, of course, but a couple of minutes at dusk when you've been up since four is always welcome. So the general tiredness wasn't doing anything to quell the mounting anxiety. Hero hadn't sounded angry about anything but his attitude had recently been so superfluous to events around him that I wondered if he was affecting a total disconnect between whatever was going on in order to retain his position as the producer and overseer. He could have been furious about something, and given the piss flying through the air and continual barking going on, he was entitled to be. David remained inscrutable rather than displaying any other overall attitude. I'd seen him be like that when things weren't going well, but he tended to meet good news and setbacks with the same cap-down mien. I had recently begun to wonder if, despite the energy he needed to keep things going day-to-day, there was anything much going on under that cap apart from incipient baldness. Had the camera lens become the face?

Anyway, there they were. David was almost horizontal on the little-ish sofa, looking like a giant action man doll that had been plopped down by a child that had found another plaything. I couldn't see his eyes, but he was happily displaying his stubbly muzzle and nasal hair. Hero was curiously energised, which made me feel all the more tired. I wondered if he was on something but there were none of the usual signs. That worried me all the more, as being in a state like that without recourse to drug was surely a sign of being crazed.

They were, however, drinking. Little bottles of lager, which I was offered and declined, although I soon realised that I couldn't have as I was actually drinking one.

-So look, you've been a great help over the last few weeks-

Oh god, was this it? Was I being fired for being sane?

-We know this hasn't been the easiest shoot for everyone so far-

David interjected, quietly, before Hero continued, loudly:

-But we know that this is a good project. We're making something special here, y'know. Once this is done and out there, and getting the attention that it deserves, We know that everyone involved will look back on it as something they're proud to have contributed to-

I must have made some kind of noise here, as they both murmured back in assent-

-That's the thing. This is why we got into this industry. Whatever tribulations come our way during any shoot just melt away when, years later, we look at the finished work, the end project, and see it for what it is. Yeah? Rather than remembering what happened – indeed, I'd be surprised if the difficult parts of a shoot really stick with anyone. Of all the work that we've done together, Lina, tell me –do you remember the difficult days?

Tired as I was, I couldn't believe I was hearing such asinine shit. I mean, really. It was the exact opposite of everything I'd experienced in my few years of shoots. Even if I did have an opportunity to re-watch some of the forlorn little films I'd knackered myself on, I know that any aesthetic virtue would be drowned out by vivid memories of scab-ridden hotel rooms, snappy would-be starlets; frenetically avoiding the gropey advances of never-gonna-be stars. That's one of the main reasons I avoid any glancing chance to see them. That's part of the reason I

avoid seeing any films at the moment. Even if I didn't work on it – and I probably didn't, if it's a film you might stand a good chance of seeing – I'd only imagine the kind of hair-raising stuff that the poor units who made it went through.

Of course I agreed with him.

What point was there in speaking my mind? I'd obviously been asked there for some purpose and with these kind of things it tends to be something that they want doing. Breaking away from their chain of thought from the start would show that you were declining to play along. And with if I'd been honest with Hero and let slip that I'm now working on these things to survive, not because I love film, or want to make some of my own, in fact the opposite; that I've come to believe that there's too many films being made and I'd be better off doing something less insane with my life, well...getting the boot at this part of the game wouldn't be a good move.

-Thanks. We know that you know that because we knew you from the start. And if, Lisa, the path hasn't led to you directing your own feature yet, I'm sorry. I know that each shoot throws up its own needs and problems. I'm a producer. I fertilise the script and bring it to fruition, I'm present throughout the labour and by god I'm there to deliver the end result. Everyone is different but we all know that there's a thousand little tasks to keep each one on course, little duties.

-It's the fact that you've been able to subsume that talent for directing and -at times, when needed, when you knew that it would help the birth of our collective child, you diligently stepped in to focus on a task that needed doing, despite the fact that you know that we know you're capable of running these joint anyway – that's what makes us acutely aware that you are made of the right stuff. You're film-maker.

With this he tilted the rest of his beer back, placed it on the small table between us, and gave an incongruously long exhalation. I felt the acidic tang of his breath reach me seconds later.

I didn't agree or disagree with this, mainly as I didn't really get what he was on about. I nodded and took a tiny sip of my beer instead.

David leaned slightly forward now, as Hero seemed to regard something outside the plasticky window to my left.

-We know you'll step up to this.

-It's something you'll be able to handle well. There's been lots of little disagreements over the last few weeks and more than some frayed tempers-

Curiously, Hero was still looking out of the window whilst addressing me.

-But I'll admit that there's one person who's methods and style of working haven't been to everyone's taste-

Fifteen resignations and a priest lamped in the face in a hotel foyer.

-And that's understandable. In many ways, it's generational. He's from a different era-

The Cretaceous?

-and we're a mostly young crew. These things have happened. And they will, in all likelihood, continue to happen. As I said earlier, all irrelevant in the long term once the film's done and out in the world. But when the problems start to blend out of the cast and crew, and into the people we find ourselves working alongside for a few weeks.

You're in a lot more trouble, because that's real life getting punched in the face?

-We're essentially putting our difficulties into the public sphere, and it's unethical of us to allow members of society – members of wider society - to suffer because of some difficulties we're having with different methods of working.

That was, I'm sure as concrete, the only time I've heard Hero use the word ethics. And I love the way he managed to undercut his own attempt at waddling onto the moral high ground by alluding to it; surely the implication of what he said was that if it's members of the crew getting punched or covered in piss then it's alright?

-So we have three weeks left. We'll complete the picture, and as I'm sure you know, everything that we have shot is looking fantastic.

The bottom line is the only line.

-But with Dermot, we're worried that he's getting increasingly unpredictable away from the camera. It's got a bit more extreme than disappearing off to a pub of an afternoon. We're worried that the next time he bolts, he might not come back, or he'll do something even more damaging to whoever gets in his way.

-So we'll need to make sure he's steered to safety. Subtly. Kept an eye on, once he's away from the set.

I'd gone very cold by this point. I swear the wind started to batter the walls harder. They didn't even have to state it.

-Why are you asking me?

-Because we have confidence that you can do it.

-We're not asking for 24-7 surveillance. This is more about putting an extra layer of responsibility onto the tasks that you have.

-Have you asked anyone else?

-No.

I still don't know if that's true. All I can do is choose to believe it. We were silent for a few seconds afterward. I guess it's a bind that most people will find themselves in at work. When the boss wants you to do something that's obviously shit, but if you decline, they may chose to decline from continuing to employ you.

-I'll need more money, if I do.

They continued to be silent. This obviously hadn't been anticipated. The wind rose in an outraged whinny.

-Er. Yeah. Of course. We'll...

-We'll double it.

Hero looked over to David, seemingly having dealt with two unexpected statements in a matter of seconds.

-From now 'till wrap. Yes, double.

That seemed fair. Well, it was what I wanted, so I guess it would.

-Alright. You're on.

And I guess that's another familiar feeling from the world of work. Dreading the task but agreeing for the money.

-Good. Now the first task will be to make sure he's back in his hotel room by seven tomorrow. It's a five a.m call the following morning, so we need to know that he's not out rampaging through or at anyone or anything beforehand.

-Uh. Ok...what do I do, lie in wait at the hotel or tag myself onto him before the day wraps?

-Inveigh yourself towards him.

-We're choosing you because you can be subtle like that, as you know. You can be around the set doing things and no-one would have a clue-

Could I? Did I? Well it wasn't deliberate, so, cheers, yeah, guys?

-So just make a reason up for yourself to stick close to him for the duration. But not close enough to arouse suspicion in him.

-Alright, well he seems pretty suspicious of pretty much everyone...

-Exactly, so that gives you good cover. If he's looking askance at all of us, you won't stand out.

-Right, so I think of something that means I'll have to be there all the time after the shoot, but including getting him to the door of the hotel-

-His room, within the hotel.

Oh Christ.

-So...right...I'm not just keeping him away from the pubs, I'm making sure he's in the room, and what – putting a bolt over the door that'll only be opened at three the next morning?

-No, look, we thought about something like that but the hotel won't customise their doors. Unless there was a lot of money being offered.

-No, you need to make sure he's in there, alright, that's when you call us on your mobile.

I'd forgotten I had their numbers. I was at the bottom of the call sheet, hadn't had any contact on that front.

-And that's when Gog and Magog will be put on sentry duty.

-What will?

-Who will?

-Gog and Magog, as he said. We've had some help from them on other projects, you remember? No? They've provided security on several night shoots when we needed to make sure that none of us would be disturbed. No, not their real names, really we don't know their real names. Don't need to.

I remembered something about two terrifying men that said little and were avoided by most people on set. Faces that looked like they'd been blasted with sandpaper from a young age, puffa jackets that gave the impression that their already intimidating physiques were expanding to make all in their orbit feel smaller than they already were in comparison.

-Them! They're going to be outside his bloody door all night? I thought we were supposed to be protecting the general public, not scaring them even more?

-Lina, cool it. It isn't like that. They'll be subtly placed outside, either side of the hotel but so that if he tries to get out, they'll see. They'll also be close enough to get in quickly if anything happens in there and resolve the situation calmly.

It was at that point that I realised that I was gradually becoming afraid of more than Mr Boyle. In fact, I wasn't sure where to start.

-Right, so they're going to be in place, do I have to signal to them? Text them?

-You won't need to, they'll see you. They'll be looking out for you, no need for you to signal anything, that'd arouse suspicion.

-In who? Dermot will be in the room by then, won't he? So how would he be able to get suspicious?

-We don't mean him.

-Then who?

-Well, if anyone else saw this going on they might think that some kind of security job was going on.

-But isn't that what will be going on?

-Yes, exactly, which is why we don't want anyone being aware of it.

-It'll compromise the security of what we're doing.

-Ok, so apart from the hotel staff...

-No, no hotel staff awareness.

-They don't know anything about this?

-Not as such, not what we've been talking about just now.

-They've been told that we're keeping Dermot under wraps alright, but that's more on your side of the operation than Gog and Magog's.

-There's degrees of detail that they need to know, and the last part isn't one of the degrees. We want them to know that we're on it, but we don't want them to feel like the production is staking the place out overnight.

-Which is essentially what we're all doing.

-Which is exactly why we can't let them know that.

-Right, I think I've got the picture.

-That's great, but remember that you can't officially know that we're doing it either.

-As far as you know, all you know is what you're doing. You don't know anything about what anyone else is doing. Because they aren't doing anything.

-But if anything does come out – you never knew about it.

-R...right.

-We're making it easier for you, all things considered. And you know that nothing will happen, anyway.

(If I'd thought that before, I wasn't by then, although I tried to look like what they'd suggested was true. It must have taken me a while to untangle my thoughts, but I know that the next thing I said was -)

-So when I've made sure he's in the room, I just walk out back to mine, job done for the night?

-Oh, you won't need to, actually. We were coming to that.

-We've moved you.

-To the hotel.

-The same hotel?

-The same floor. Room 16c.

-Just around the corner, not right by.

-When you say moved –it's already done?

-No, well, you'll need to get your stuff from the boarding house. We haven't gone near that.

-Wait. If you've got it done already –what if I'd said no? What if I still say no?

-Well...we wanted you to have a better room either way.

-We know you've been putting everything into your efforts to keep the ship running, so we wanted you to have a calmer berth for the remainder.

-I was going to get the room even if I said no just now.

-Probably. But we knew you wouldn't say no, because that isn't the kind of thing you'd do.

-And you didn't.

-Yes, you didn't.

-So it's not worth worrying about any more.

-I'll just worry about this other factor instead.

-Nothing to worry about, honestly. It's important alright – for all parties involved. But it's a soft touch. More likely, it'll be an extra task to clock off before you get back to a clean bed every night.

-And don't think we won't make a note of this for next time. Directing, producing, it's all about working with the circumstances that occur around you and moulding them into what they need to be.

-And we know you've been able to do well with everything else, so...

-Are you saying this may stand me in good stead for directing in the future?

-Well, it's not something you've mentioned to us recently, but...

-We were wondering if you were just happy to help out. Ah, integral as those tasks are, of course.

-Yes, although we didn't want to broach the subject for you, if you want to take this on I'm sure it can act as a catalyst to grabbing a bigger nettle for the next shoot.

-You have to develop, after all. One can't be passive in this arena. So think of this as a ladder. We've thrown a ladder at you.

-Down for you.

-Whatever. It's a ladder. And it's there now.

The wind outside was continuing to build. I could see sand and twigs careering past the Winnebago's windows.

-So whilst we can't guarantee anything –we can't guarantee ourselves anything, in this industry, after all, we know as well as you do that if you're able to do this, you're able to do anything. This isn't a production in need of saving, but you can save it nonetheless.

-Take as long as you like to decide about this, by the way. It's your decision.

-Although as you can guess, we need to get this ball rolling tomorrow, so we'll need to know soon.

-Kind of now, really. And you've said you're up for it, so can we count that as done?

I murmured something. I was seeing double, due to exhaustion more than the little I'd had to drink. My eyelids were getting heavy on the blurry vision of four men staring back at me over the busy little table.

-Good.

-Great, even!

-Very glad that you've come round to this.

Their energy didn't seem to have sapped at all. I remember raising myself to pointlessly shake their hands and stepping out, pulling my hood up as the door opened onto a cold blast and the kind of deep black night that you can only get when very far away from London. How much of what had just happened I'd agreed to, I couldn't be sure. I only knew that I'd found myself in a shitty scenario.

Silly me. Id've run away, run home, if I could only remember where that was.

Fuck me, weird news travels fast in situations like these.

I knew something was up when I arrived at the catering for my first and, it turned out, only caffeine of the day. It was just before five, they had a few set ups to get through that day and the first was an interior, in some bungalow that the scout had found, already overstuffed with eccentric bric-a-brac; this would serve as the old geezer' house. It fit the bill so perfectly that little alterations needed to be done. Saving on time effort and money, bang on target for the meagre budget the company had managed to squeeze out from god-knows-where.

The catering van was parked up in some grassy non area a few minutes walk away. As was the custom then, our teas and snacks were being served in a repurposed double-decker bus which was on loan from some other, bigger company. In the dark its windows were still yellow against the encroaching light, its bulk massive and incongruous amongst the squat little bungalows spread unevenly around.

I was one of the first there, some sparks and costume had arrived and were huddled around a portable heater on the lower deck.

-Morning Lorna.

-Hi.

I wasn't sure if they'd got my name wrong or if they were slurring with tiredness. By now we were all going to bed tired and arriving tired. Caffeine allowed us to function throughout the day's work. I'd walked back through the dark the night before and here I was turning up with darkness still around.

I made my way to the counter, which was behind the driver's booth. A chubby greaser handed me a Styrofoam cup of coffee, and gave me a look. And a statement-

-That's brave of you.

-Uh –sorry, what?

-Volunteering like that. Good on you! Sugar.

I was about to tell him not to call me sugar when I realised he was offering me some. I took a spoonful and asked-

-Volunteering for what?

-Protection. Sorry, bacon rolls are on–need to go out back.

I'd never seen that man before. I stood alone with the coffee. It was currently the only warmth getting through to me. The too-loud voices from the table had stopped. I turned to them.

-Morning. What?

They'd barely heard the first syllable of 'morning' before they'd dropped their stares down to the wooden table between them.

-Oh, just remembered that you're tired?

-Just don't want to stare.

Piped up the bigger one, a hairy bloke squeezed into the chair, his belly was pushed out over the table like bristly play-dough.

-Oh, well...that's polite of you.

I lifted the coffee up and took a sip. It felt so hot that I didn't know whether to hold it in my mouth to try and wake myself up with the scorching heat, or spit it onto the bus' floor for fear of scalding my tongue beyond the power of speech. It took a couple of seconds before I realised I was trying to decide what to do, and by then I'd gagged it down anyway. I stood coughing by the counter, swaying slightly and wondering if I was about to sick up in front of these people.

-He's right though, it is very brave of you.

-What? What is, wearing this coat?

-No,' croaked some angular make up girl, who couldn't have been over 21, 'no, wearing that's just dumb.

-Thwashn't mahqwuestion!

Oh god, I was slurring. I needed more coffee. Which would stop the slurring, but almost certainly make me sick.

-Alright! Fuck.

Hairy man again.

-Jesus. Cool it, the day hasn't even started yet. You can't blame people if they react when you volunteer to do something as daft as that.

-People will say stuff, you know. (A young girl, visibly trying to think of what to say.) -I mean, with all that's gone on since we've been here, the thought that someone would volunteer to try and look after him...

-I didn't...

-Didn't you?

-I did.

-Then why did you? (Fat man).

Why had I? What could I say, that it had been suggested before I knew what was going on? That the alternative looked like being fired and never working again? No. Well, they probably knew it themselves, if they had an inch of imagination or empathy between them. Which there was, of course, no guarantee of.

-Well, at least it's me and not you.

-I'd thought that, actually.

-Oh. Well. Great. Look, we all know what a nightmare it's been, particularly him. I'll be trying to keep him away from people off-set, not you. You can't escape each other. We've got weeks left, and if he goes on the rampage and maims anyone again this whole shoot could be shut down. So I'm keeping you in a job, right?

That's great, isn't it? My first reaction was to couch the whole thing in terms of our pay. Still, it was the only thing that looked like working.

-Right. Like we said, very brave. (Weaselly man who hadn't piped up yet). 'Good luck between now and the wrap.

-Thanks. Thanks? Thanks.'

-Anyway. We've got to be on set with Zephiah. Long scene, and apparently she hasn't been sleeping well.

-Who has?

-Right, but she's the one in front of the camera.

I emitted some kind of assertive gurgle as they left. Teflon Zephiah, we hadn't heard so much as a for fuck's sake from all her all this time. Surely something was going on back there? Perhaps that was what was keeping her awake. Being tolerant all this time. I looked back at the counter. No sign of anyone. I could have done with more caffeine – everyone could always do with more caffeine on a set, especially this one –but I walked out and towards the set-up.

-Laura Butler, what a nutter! Da da da, da da d a da!

-Fuck off! (It was Len, one of the cameramen, who was combining his singing, or bellowing, rather, with some kind of knock-kneed gyration. This, coupled with the sight of his flabby, bell-shaped head, was really too much to take.)

-No, nice one, but why...

-Fuck off, I said!

-Can't. Have to stay here and get the shoot done. So what's the deal, are you being his bodyguard or fluffer.

-Shut up! Shut up and fuck off!

-Well, I can do one of them, eventually. Seriously, are you getting danger money for this?

Didn't know what to say to that. I hadn't known what to say to his previous comments, but I knew even less now. Essentially, I was. I'd demanded it, and they'd conceded to it. I couldn't let people know this. It's one thing to be doing an impossible job that will ensure that you're openly mocked. People will want you around, to make sure it isn't them at the top of the mockery list, it'll make them feel dignified by default. But it's another thing to be getting extra money for it. No-one will thank you for that.

I said nothing, but noise was still coming out of my mouth. Some sort of fading yodel. My arms were doing something as well, going up and down as if they were patting an invisible dog in mid-air. I turned on my heel and swerved away, then realised I was going in the wrong direction, and swerved back. I had made myself dizzy. A male voice piped from somewhere unseen-

-No dancing at this time of morning, please.

-Fuck off!

I was sure I was going to be sick.

I headed to the honeywagon, which was further down the road, parked up near some Volvos. Emma from continuity was coming out, squinting at the emerging light;

-Morning, Laura. Your charge has just entered make-up.

Christ! How did everyone know? And so soon? I'd barely gotten used to the fact myself and now everyone on set knew, well-

Everyone? Did he? Now, of course our two overlords would not want the man himself to know someone had been given a specific role to keep him away from the general public, it would surely defeat the action of getting someone to do it. But if the fact had already travelled around the crew, could we know for sure that it wouldn't somehow slip out to the subject himself?

Well. The very facets of Dermot's mad personality that had gotten him into this mess would surely work in our-my-favour. There really didn't seem to be any communication between him and the rest of the people working on the film, bar the direction from David, and he was at one remove to the rest of the grunts. No, I couldn't imagine one of the make-up girls accidentally blabbing about the shenanigans to him whilst trying to make his skin look less grey one morning. I couldn't imagine one of the make-up girls making small talk of any kind with him, considering how freaked out by him they said they were. And they're prize talkers, I think they do it to set themselves and their subjects at ease more than anything. I've known them to get a good conversation out of an actor who subsequently turned out to have been asleep.

Not that we could really tell if this one was asleep or awake, or somewhere between both. Don't know if he knew either, or cared.

By now I couldn't even be bothered to rebuke Emma for knowing about my new role. Waste of energy I didn't have.

-Great. Has anyone said how he is?

-Usual muttering to himself. Smells of aftershave and strong, cheap booze. Good luck, eh?

-Thanks. Right.

After managing to keep my coffee down I walked to the set –the bungalow – passing the make up van. I heard laughter. His, and his alone. Well, you'd never mistake it for that of a make-up girl. Distinctively his, rasping, on the verge of cracking like old dry leaves underfoot. And mirthless, more the sound of someone recognising a bitter truth rather than any kind of joy.

I walked by. Down the hill toward the house, I saw a bottle by a bench. One of those cheap cider bottles, fat like a little plastic warhead, open and mostly empty, right under the harsh metal bench. The kind of drink favoured by unfortunates, destitutes, people with problems.

Not that I'd seen any around this town. No, bleak as it was, if Bitchington Little or Greater – had any homeless people, they were well out of sight. Which made me think, who...

...well, who else. Not that I'd have thought his habits were that extreme. But there seemed to be no other explanation, unless someone in the crew had started hitting pre-morning cider heavily as a result of having to work with him. Mind, if they had they'd be sure of getting fired. Unlike him.

I looked closer. Dribble down the side, still running down to the pavement. Fresh. I checked my watch, and had to press the button to light the neon backing. Quarter past six.

This time I really was sure I was going to heave.

Bright. Ugh, bright light against my eyeballs. And sand, more of the bleedin' sand, flies around everywhere in this little town. Which is, Dermot dear? Can't remember. Wait –

Since when have I been staring at the sea? And are those seals I can hear moaning on about something or other?

I'm sat down on another of those benches, seems. It's one of the steel ones, I realise now, as my arse is cold. Jeez, the light, squinting isn't enough between that and the sand on the breeze. Look down.

Right. Now. You're definitely still in the town because you've been here before, some hillock near the seafront. I'm the pillock on the hillock, alright? Good, still coming up with this kind of word-nonsense when I should be sorting the situation out. What's there to sort out?

Well, how did you get here and what were you doing beforehand? This is the most urgent question, as currently it's the most mysterious. We wrapped late in the evening and...

Ah yes, the shoot. The shoot. Daylight. I'm sure I read on the sheet that I'm not needed for this day. Is that right? If it isn't, I may have ballsed up everything altogether. No, I'm sure if there's one thing I remember correctly it's that they'll be shooting with the young one today and they don't need my services. That's hoping that today is still today and isn't yesterday now, that I haven't blacked out up here and missed a day entirely. No. Unlikely.

Those bloody seals. What is it, no fish to find? Shut it.

Sharp intake of breath. Cold. Not as cold as I should be, try to move arms, and-hey-ah. Wondered what that weight was, only just sensed it now. The reliable old Yellow Lightning bottle. Cradled in my lap, snout pointed out toward the sea, sniffing for France. Don't blame it, myself. Fairly weighty, yes, around a half-bottle left now. Good measure for whatever time we have left. Can't exert myself to unto the cap at present though, perhaps it's too early for breakfast.

Yes, and not as cold as I feel I should be...ah. Coat. I'm wearing a big old coat here, yes, hood up and all, now I wonder if that helped me stay asleep over-well, could have been minutes or hours but I'm guessing I've been out a while. This may have helped me ward off pneumonia, provided this is where I've been all the time. It's a great coat, this. I wonder who's it is. Well, was. I think we'll get on great together. Wonder where the cider came from, too. Well, I have a good way of finding it, no, it finds its way to me. Wonder if it was the same owner of both? What happened to them? No, what happened to me, I'm the one living this, fuck any others.

Nothing is returning to the film-reel of my mind. The takes have been lost, oh crew.

God, look at it. Slate sea, clouds skimming away from up behind me way out to the ocean so quickly. Poetic, Dermot! If predictable. A lone drunk finds beauty in the view he wakes up to. I've woken to worse. Edge of England. That's what it feels like. No, I can't have been the first to think of a place being that, but it does, feels like I'm out of the edge of the country, few years behind London, this place, from what I remember. No bad thing, I feel at home in the past.

What year is it? Now? If this place is in the past, I'll have to remember what the present is in order to get my bearings. Well the century turned and a few years ago, that's for sure. That was the new year party that carried on for so long it could have been for two years' worth. Two thousand and three. No, four. Not five yet, surely? All improbable years, doesn't feel right to be alive in whatever year it is. Sci-fi years, really. Consider yourself lucky, Boyle, you made it this far when many did not. Still alive and in some kind of employment, improbably.

I swear those seals sound closer. Seals. Weird, never really given them much thought. Like blubbery dogs, really. Hang on. Not carnivorous, I hope. Never read anything in the papers about some poor gobshite having his or her kneecaps ripped off by a bunch of marauding seals, did I? No, I am sure I did not.

Either way, never seen a quick seal on anything, one of those documentaries or the like. No, I'm safe up here.

Wait. Is that the bench's cold on my arse or did I...did I piss myself again? Again? Can't remember the last time I did that but I do know it's happened, even back in my adult life. Please, no, I seem to have come to in a good situation, don't let my bladder have relaxed too much when I was out. Put the bottle under one arm there, steady it. Right, slide the other down between trouser and bench's steel. Fuck, god it's cold and stiff. My hand. Purple, I bet, but I don't want to look right now. Priority is the potential piss question. Later.

Hmm. No. Inconclusive at best. I'm just cold all over. Hard to tell. If it happened, it happened during the night and it's as good as absorbed now. Good as new! Maybe. Yes, it's just that I'm frozen to shit all over and on a steel bench, with the wind blasting me. If it had been more recent, if it was what woke me up perhaps, it'd be giving a feeling of heat. In fact...yes. I haven't pissed myself. But I am about to. Bladder feels like a heavy melon. Fit to blow.

Now let's see. I now have to deal with the first decision of the day. Early on for such things, but I find myself in exceptional circumstances. Now. Option one. I sit here and warm myself up by bringing some recycled cider into the world. Two. I make a run for it and try to find some public bog or otherwise secluded impromptu pissoir to relieve myself otherwise.

Don't pretend that you haven't done it before, Boyle. You should be an expert on these things by now. Right. Run for it? Well, I can't really run for it as I can't really run at all nowdays, let's face it. Body, not up for it. Frail. Although –what? What did I do some other night? Something physical, not...no. Thrown punch at someone? Connected? Some oul fella, some older fella, rather? No. Can't have. Bury that one, come back to it later when this has been sorted. Time is running out along with bladder control.

So, the sit down option. Sit here and piss meself and get a bit warm in the process. There are drawbacks to this, I acknowledge. I'd be sitting in a pool of my own piss, for one. Not ideal. But warm. No. Warmth can be found in other places, lummox! Dignity, come on. Look. Back over behind, to where the town will inevitably be, unless it slid into the sea overnight, which would be impossible, I hope. No, it's there. Not much on this stretch, bland houses. Probably for those of my age who worked, saved for pensions, and now find themselves in warm houses with their own toilets. Maybe I could ask one? Hello, good morning, my name is Dermot, you may recognise me from various heavy roles in undistinguished TV productions of the last few decades, in my youth I was cursed with promise but I have found myself awake in the beach in front of your house, yes that very one you're familiar with, in a stranger's coat and I've also pinched a big bottle of cider which has made me need a big wee. Whilst I hope this isn't a regular occurrence for you, would you deign to let a washed-up actor toot in your loo, please? Promise not to fuck your poodle, if you have one.

Uh? Oh, lost myself there. No, unlikely at best, and may alert me to the authorities. If there are any around here. Wait-something else? Recent, something with police, or someone dressed like that, called out. Hotel? Something I was involved in? Ah, no, just an ambulance crew, perhaps, something that had gone on and I'd chanced over it. Must think...it'll come back. Task in hand.

Yes, this. Time still running out, that's what it does. Is this a true dilemma, I wonder. Sit and stew in myself here and inevitably get discovered my some biddy, or strike out and get discovered doing the biz by a trolley? No, one is better. Get on the move and see what the day holds. Perhaps find a darker corner to enjoy this stuff in peace. Provided they don't need me.

Dunes! Of course, you prannet, the dunes will have enough cover for you somewhere. Bottle can be secured in the sand and coat opened for when the stream is freed. So. Up, come on. Balance. Oh god, the light, don't know which is harder, that or the sand whipping into me. Uh. Looks like I'm up, swaying slightly, but here I am. Dizzy, alright, ride it out. Hold left hand in front and stare at it, you look nuts whilst doing it but it reduces the dizz. Done! Learned that in the seventies and it still works. OK. Set off, right foot into the sand, slowly but keep that intent. I seem to have lost a sock at some juncture. No bother, task in hand is not being affected. Squint as best you can, bottle secure. Both arms around it now. Guess I could act like it's a child or small dog and I'm carrying it across the dunes for a dip. If pressed to explain myself.

Those bloody seals, they're incessant. Uncanny echo to them. I never liked hearing things I can't see. Guess they're down by the water though. I don't remember any stories of seals owning houses, so –

Ah. Come back to that thought some other time you fool, you're about to burst. Waddle over to the deeper dune dip over there, away from the wind and any potential prying eyes, oh hell now the thought of having to display what's left of the old feller to the world. Well what else am I to do, piss through a hole in the trousers?

This is fierce. Right, think I've got a good balance going, bladder is primed, just void all you need to and torrent out rather than doing the stop-start dribbling thing that you were pulling the other night, will you please? We'll have to get this done quickly before humanity gets a chance to see, and I've given you at least an hour to build up momentum.

Jeez, here we go. Uh. Not had one like this in a long time, hell, feels like I could be here till nightfall. Well, I know something's still down there of some description, after all what else would I be pissing out of? It's turning the sand lumpen and peaty. Smells and indeed looks just like the stuff was when it came in. Right, the sandy trough is overflowing, driddling down the dune. Let it go, it'll dry soon enough, and by then I'll be well away. Indoors, at least.

Uh, now how long have I been stood like this, I wonder. Doesn't feel like it's going to stop at any time soon. Hopefully I'm just getting rid of the half-bottle here, feels like I may be passing some minor entrails as well if this doesn't ebb. Ah now, its scattering down over the dune like a dark octopus in all directions. Black against the white sand, very ostentatious. Not what I need now.

Come on! Is that...right, I think it's slowing. Its course is almost done. Voided. Ok, better re-breech myself, I'm feeling ready for a drink after all that exertion. And still, the seals. Closer, it sounds. No time for reverie, get that zip done and find the bottle, there it is, up with you-

Oh-

That seal noise isn't coming from a seal, I see a man shape. I think the man shape has clocked me, coming over from the direction of the shore, ah, ah no. He's seen the used cider trails, and now, yes-he's looking right at myself, and those are very angry noises, man not seal, and there seem to be more following. Up from where he came from. Agitated, looking-hm, looking just as rough as I probably do. Now, gentlemen, what has brought you here, perhaps you were enjoying a morning by the waves yourself and have come to christen the day?

Something is slightly familiar about this lot, could it? Hm, best not to find out, I'm starting to feel, something down below is shrivelling as much as it can do, I think I may have to follow its lead and disappear, sharpish.

Yes, they're starting to accelerate, well, much as they can, in a stumbling fashion, lumbering with the menace of a recently-woken mummy in some old black and white shocker. Similar grumpy intent. No, all eyes are now on me and the expressions I'm making out are the wrong side of grumpy.

Run!

Oh you old fool, don't die like this, will you, running from a group of vagrants on a godforsaken nowhere at the edge of England with a bottle of cheap cider in your arms. Not a runner at the best of times nowdays, and it seems that sand just isn't a surface I should be competing in. They sound fairly far back, down the dunes, must be near the piss-trough now, where can I get to for god's sake? Quick look back. Gaining, still moving, can almost make out the shouting, all purpose English shouting, words garbled but noise stating violent intent.

Now did I notice that one of them wasn't wearing a coat? Yes, I may have. Could have something to do with their fury. If I did manage to subtly borrow it, I'd quite happily hand it back. I don't want anyone dying of pneumonia on my watch. But that goes for me above all else. And I think the time for politely handing it back has gone, somehow.

Made it to the top of the dunes! How? Feel like the lungs are about to burst but here I am. Turn. They're down but gaining, I'm guessing they're more used to a night under the stars than I, and they're waking up. Street near. Good. Distract them somehow. Joke? No. Know your audience, fool. If I can get into the town I can given them the slip, I'd reckon, on even ground. Plan! The bottle?

Oh, come on, really? Yes, only option, alas. And I see no refreshments being carried by them. This may be another piece of the puzzle, if I have angered them by making away with their booze then it is time to make it go back to where it came from. Lift! That's it, above the head, wielding it like that ape with the bone at the start of the Kubrick film-

That's it, lads, one of yours, I presume? They've clocked it all right, so time to send it underarm, good swing there old bean, out it goes, curving through the air, explosion of sand as it hits the duneside. Reaction, alright, two of them have lunged for it.

'Cheers!'

Now there was no need to shout that out, you old fool. They'll only think you're being sarky. Time to turn and run-

Oh, feels like I'm hit by a brick there, ah, no. Spent too long flouncing about and didn't see the initial one sidle up by me, must've slapped me up back of the head. Hood broke the impact? Oh, yes, shouting in my face with a methsy blast of gut-air. Weathered. Stubbly. May have seen him recently, alright. Flesh like corned beef. No, spam. Spam-man. Enough, he's moving to lunge again, so-

Ah god, how'd you manage to do it so well still, and in your state? Still capable of surprising myself, it seems. Duck, sweep a spindly leg twixt his, shove the chin at the same time just so he's off-centre, and down he goes, bellowing still, careering down the mound to his friends.

And by then I'm off.

Worzel Gummywhatsisname taught me that one, you know. Sad that I'll never get the chance to pass it on myself. And instinct taught me the follow-up, which is to have leapt into a garden and buried myself in a hedge. Must still be early, I see few people out , so I'll have a good chance of scuttling from garden to garden before I can reach whatever semblance of a centre this town has. I see the name now as I huddle inauspiciously amongst rhododendrons. Looks like I was just outside the city limits, sign says-

You are now entering

BITCHINGTON

Please drive safely.

Yes, the name has come back to me. Bitchington. Ending my career in Great Bitching. A fond farewell. And all this with some free booze having been dispensed as collateral to make sure I'm not beaten before breakfast. Still, nice to know I'm not an alcoholic. There's no way an alkie would have gotten rid of free booze like that.

You can certainly tell a lot about a town by shuffling around its bushes of a morning. Very genteel, this, barely a used rubber or scorched porno about the place. Really, I'm being treated to a nice work-out of a morning. Haven't had the knees and elbows work like this in a long time. Well, they seem to still be working, barely, even if inwardly I'm...not with the world.

No. Enough of that for now, try and think of that – if you have to, at all – once you're back at base and safe. Not foraging around Bitchington, if that's what it calls itself. Right, that's another sign coming up on the corner, I can see that white on green lettering, dive low and crawl toward the corner, there's a low wall to grab hold of. Ah good, I seem to have done so, and now I'll follow by pulling myself up over the wee wall, clear of the bush, over and-

Shit!

-Headfirst onto the pavement, it seems. Well, I'm here, and that's the main thing. Some screaming, it seems. Ah yes, seem to have emerged near some kids on the way to school. Ok, weekday morning it is. That is positive news. May have frightened some small children by emerging head-first from a hedge. That is, potentially, very bad news.

'Nothing to worry about here, kids. Just doing some early morning gardening.'

There. Well, they're moved away, for sure. I think I got all of that out clearly, although as my jaw is somewhat cold and I hadn't adequately prepared it may be that some of the vowels and indeed consonants emerged in a less than coherent manner. No matter. I see the sign. One way for the crazy golf, the other directly to the town centre, ah yes, nice of Little Bitching to have a centre and to tell me about it. Time for a quick ruffle of the hair, may have picked up some detritus on the way here. Indeed, there goes quite a lot of soil, and indeed a worm. Back in the bushes for you, my legless friend. Can't be bringing you into the hotel as a guest. We don't want to try their patience, after all.

Hm. Crazy golf. Now something else is swimming back to me. Perhaps a venue for last night? Possible. Definitely trod on some kind of false grass last night. Is that the term? False grass, plastic grass, something. Can't be much of it around this place, I'd guess. Well, no matter you dead fool, just get to where you need to be, wherever that happens to be. God, what does the hotel look like? White façade, Edwardian at a guess. Well done, that narrows it down. If there's more than one of them in this place I may be fucked. Now why am I still staring at the sign? Oh. Town centre two miles this way, so it says.

Two miles. Even in my sprightly morning state, this is too much of a stretch. You'll surely agree that I've had a challenging morning already. Legs are wobbling, there. Hand down on the wall for a moment. Allow the dizziness to subside.

There. Now. God, the light. Closing my eyes, all I can see are angry pulses of pink and purple. Other hand to the brow, there. God, an appreciable amount of sweat. Cold to the touch. Look down at that hand. Rivulets of it running over a shaky paw, dirt ingrained in my palm lines, my fingerprints. Sorry sight, altogether. Ok. Legs are steadier, dizziness gone. Plan? Yes, taxis have been seen somewhere in this town, I've seen them pass

when giving the youth the slip after the day's wrap. White, with brown markings. That's right, oh god it's good to still notice things, eh? Useful, in case you find yourself in some kind of predicament like this. And I have now, this much I know.

So, find some taxi somewhere, they'll be crowded about some opportune area, some unofficial rank, that's what they always do. Where the trade will be waiting. Stations! A train or bus station, yes, the former, you've been to the one here, it's where you met the young shite director on the first night here. Now think harder. Near the seafront, it was, yes, couple of streets away from the beach, almost, so – follow the seafront down further into town. Not much town at all in that direction, just the crazy golf course, best avoided anyway. And best avoid the beach itself, for speed and as it seems to be the domain of the seal-voiced men. Keep in the conurbation, out of sight. Can't be more than a half-mile down to that neck of the woods, I can do that, can't I, keeping myself unobtrusive? I surely can.

And would any shoot be going on en route? Ah, question there. No, no, if today is when I think it is (no guarantee of that, but bury that thought for now, nothing you can do if it isn't and you're needed, you tragic old ruin)

If! No, no I know the schedule backwards, more than I can recall my brother's face (don't dwell on that either will you, because you know it's true), they're nowhere near the town, they'll be on the downs doing some bollix with the starlet. So I'm safe, but...stay subtle. Not just the seal men you have to avoid, it's best not to get into any random strife whatever time of the day, and whatever the reason, or lack of. Half mile or so. Think of that, stay under the shade of the merciful trees, whoah and keep an exploratory paw out to steady oneself against their trunks or the little walls. Baby steps, it's been a daft wake up after all.

Think of the bar. Not too early to crave a sit down there on the usual stool with a pot of something cold in front of me. No, that's a nice vision to keep floating in front of me for the while. Ah but, shame I had to jettison the cider (it was cider, wasn't it?), could do with it now, throat is parched from all the...cider (and what else, what else was going down there last night, there's recriminations of more coming up that desiccated bark that makes up the inside of your throat now, for sure). Nope. Carry on bravely without it, it got you into trouble and out of trouble, what more can you ask of it? There will be more, just need to get back to the room and that wad of pink and red fifties-

Uh! Money. Any cabbie will need that, and they'd want to see that as soon as you get in the car. No use promising to run out and get it in a sec on arrival, I've pulled that trick too often, so often I'd probably forget I wasn't doing it and run out and dozed off in the room. Wait. Ok, whatever form of trouser I'm wearing has pockets, and there's a twenty in the right one. Good. Permission to travel.

Stop thinking about what happened or imagining what did or didn't happen last night, it's irrelevant now, probably, and aren't you used enough to this kind of predicament? Just get to safety, is the main thing, and find out what day in time this is. And if it isn't, if it isn't your free day, if you're needed and have been and they're already looking for you all around, calling your useless little phone thing, what then?

No. Shut up. Hand to eyes, give me some back when I close them this time. Other hand on this little wall. No. You wouldn't have gone out like that, searching out for wrong to do, whatever took your mood, or presented itself, not when you knew you were needed the next day. Not even you, not even now in this last state of yours.

Surely? Really, do I think so much of myself. Surely if the decades racing away from you now tell you anything it's that there's no line you won't cross. No self-defeat too catastrophic. No let-down too jaw dropping that you won't find yourself doing it eventually. Yes, yes, but now? Now that I know it's the final one? Final. No chance of anything else springing from it, no only this as an epilogue, some last chance taken by young twerps who loved you in something god-awful that you can barely remember making and hated the one time you saw it, decades ago.

Oh, you've been handed a little miracle alright, pray you haven't fucked up the chance to make some kind of amends with yourself and money to enjoy the last days alone with. Christ, am I crying? No. Salt in the eyes from the sea breeze. Yes, still good at lying to yourself, done it so long you don't know any differ at the self-convincing gambit.

What was that, now? Enough, I'm fine and I have a task to do. And down the little hill, I saw a white and brown car drive by. Yes, another. Destiny found. Still no-one around. No-one I can see, at least. I'm sure there's a few old gimmers looking out of their windows at me. Fine, do so, you old toads, I've had a lifetime of being looked at by people I'll never see and behaving shamelessly nonetheless. Bet I'm livening up your morning. Spoiling your morning crumpet, perhaps, but it'll be a conversation. Perhaps the only one you have today.

Right. And I was right, here I am in the main stretch. Traffic and gulls is what I'm hearing, no sign of them beforehand. Civilisation, of a kind, then.

And the taxis, there's a few all bunched up together and juddering, ready for action. A couple of paunchy middle aged blokes stood by their cars, chatting away in the morning glare. Odd to think they're younger than me, they must be. Well, most people are, maybe even the codgers who were no doubt gawping at me earlier. No more. Get ready.

Hang on. You haven't taken a look at yourself today. Or indeed yesterday, at least after the make up and continuity girls had worked on you. Having woken up on a beach and spent the night doing something or other with cheap drink, it may be a safe bet that you're looking a bit alarming to civilised eyes. It may help your case if you can remedy this to the best of your abilities. After all, people seem to be rather alarmed at the sight of you even without the above extra embellishments.

There. Shop window, move over and take a look at your reflection, it's the right side of the road, the sun will pick you out.

And now I wish it hadn't. I seem to have rubbed my face in sand and shit and what's left of my hair has had enough and is trying to levitate away from my skull. There is, even an eternal optimist like me can see, probably very little I can do to beautify myself in these circumstances. Where are those make up girls when you really need them?

Ah, fuck 'em. Muster up some spit – go on, there's a bit left in there, mixed with something-or-other. Rub it on the hands and then spread evenly across the hair and face.

Now look in the window again. Not bad for a temporary measure. Almost back to normal. Not that that would do much for you, but in the immediate context...serviceable. Now you have to prepare to talk. With some coherence. Wait. Before that. Where do I need to get to, what's the name of the bloody hotel? Grand. No, Seafront. Oh god, looks like a description may be necessary. More words. More hurdles.

Almost at the ranks now. Legs are still feeling solid underneath me but it must be another mile and half to the blessed place so this is the only real option, Boyle.

-Good morning. Oh Christ that sounded like goo gurning, you idiot. They're looking perturbed already.

-Can you take me up to the main hotel, please? Bit better, but sounded like men hotel. So they're probably thinking that you're asking for something poofy and illicit.

-Ok. (Taller one, looking more worried than anything.) -Take it you mean the King's?

The King's! Of course it's the fucking King's, you're in middle England, everything's a fucking King or Queen thing around these places.

-Yes! Yes, the King's, that's it! (That came out more coherently, but very loudly. You are definitely sounding crazed, you old fool.)

-Sure, not too far you know. Only up that way.

What the hell is this, a cabbie trying to diddle himself out of a fare?

-It'll do me. I've been walking a while, er (you're pausing there) as you can tell. Need to get back fairly quickly.

Well that made sense to me, so what the fuck are they looking at? Oh. The clothes.

-Looks like you been out a while.

-I've been camping. (No, why did you say that? If you've been camping why the hell are you saying you need to get to a hotel?) But the wind got up and blew my tent away so....(Oh look just carry on, they've marked you down as a mental case already but as long as they can tell you can pay they'll take you.)

-So you've booked up there already?

-Uh, yes, I phoned already and they have enough of a room. Enough room. In a room for me. Look, how much will it be? I have a tenner here...

-That'll do you. Get in the back and we won't take long.

That's all you really needed to know, so here we go. Ah! Plastic covering on the back seat, the driver's protection and inebriate's insurance. Ok, we're moving.

-Good time of day for it, not much traffic.

Oh lord, does he really need to make more conversation? Is the fecker that lonely?

-Uh-no, I'd guess not. It'd be weird.

Hmm. I seem to be getting a look from him. Slight askance. What I've just said isn't any more weird than anything else I've spouted over the last few minutes. Oh. Oh no, it's not that, is it, it's one of those looks.

I've been recognised. Improbably, he seems to have clicked that he's seen me in something, at some point. This hasn't happened in a good time now. But I know that look. Good or bad things can come of it. We'll see.

-Now, I must say, I have seen you in something, haven't I?

Well, there's the rear-view-mirror? Oh don't act the prick straight off.

-Very good, no, it was on TV a while back

Yes, yes I daresay it was a good while back.

-John Thaw beat you up. Professionals, wasn't it?

Christ, was it? John Thaw may have beaten me up, but did it happen in front of a camera?

-Ah well, yes, you know you're right, I mean it was a long time ago...

-Ah no, heh, well that's brilliant. So I take it you're working on the film here then?

Christ, they've seen us about. Looks like you're still famous in your half-afterlife, ye old buzzard. -Ah, god, yes, that's us, I mean...me. Yes, couple of weeks to go.

-Anyone famous in it?

-Ah, well, if you mean famous now, no. Well, there's an actress who is, apparently. But I don't really know who's famous now. (Or even still alive and famous, is the brutal truth.)

-Right, thought it wouldn't be a blockbuster if it was being shot around here.

_It's more of an arty film. British-made, one of the TV channels is financing it. (For pity's sake, how did I getting on to talking about how cheap the gig is when I should be enjoying some glory? Still, if I talk up the lack of money maybe I'll get a free ride out of this.)

-That's why you were camping, then?

(Oh god, the camping.) -Yes, yes indeed. We're kind of on our uppers here, you see. That's most film-making for you, though. Can only afford hotels for a part of the shoot.

-And you said you even booked the place yourself?

(Fuck, I did say that, didn't I). -Well, when I said I, I meant my people. Person. People. Couldn't phone from the tent.

Well, any admiration reflected in the rear-view mirror seems to have seeped into outright concern. Back to being an object of pity. My natural state.

-I see.

Meaning he doesn't, that very little of what I've just said makes any sense to him and that it has the definite pong of on-the-fly-bullshit.

-Here it is.

I look at the meter. Six fecking pounds, but what else was I to do? That's a pint and a bit down the drain already, then. So much for a day off...if it is. Stop! No. It is. Find a note...there.

-There you go.

-That's a twenty. D'you have anything smaller?

-Ah, no sorry.

-Right.

He's fumbling about in various pouches for the change. What, am I supposed to ask him to do, keep the rest? He produces a tenner and some coins. I have no strength left to check over what's been handed back.

-Cheers.

-Yeah, no problem. I'll look out for it.

Keep your eyes peeled, you'll be lucky to find it anywhere other than collecting dust in an editing room, if my gut's on the money.

-Thanks. Hey, it'll be a while before this is out anywhere, you know.

-I'll look, sounds like the kind of stuff I like. And – sorry, I didn't catch your name.

I tell him, after I've given it a second or two's thought. I have to do that, weirdly. I immediately wish that I hadn't, as he looks utterly vacant whilst obviously searching around for a crumb of recognition.

-Don't worry, it'll come to you.

There's a lie. And then he's off, leaving me wobbling in the sun.

I made it to the room fairly quickly there, everyone working in the hotel seemed too busy to acknowledge my presence. It's fine, I knew where I was going. Once in the room I lobbed all the night's accrued gear into some kind of kit bag that I seem to have been bequeathed recently, gave my face and hair a soaping in the bathroom, and checked the call sheet. Left where I always leave it, on the dresser under the room's Gideon bible, which seems to have been mildly blasphemed recently, I guess by the current inhabitant.

Yes, you old fool. Breathe easily, it says you're not needed. And the little plastic phone that you see by the sheet, there's nothing on it, it's blank, no little signs or half-hidden sentences for you on the little green screen. Little toy-like thing, supposed to have it by my side at all times, they said when they gave it to me. No. No, thanks, just one more nasty little method of making one permanently to hand. Stay there, little tonka phone, unless I feel like shoving you somewhere to make a point.

Ah, it seems that I'm crying with relief. So that was me being blaze about knowing I was off, wasn't it? No certainty at all. No, you just woke up from another random blackout with no real conception of the how, the why, the where. And you aren't in control at all, not the slightest, even when you know that this is the last one, the job that's come in the final stretch of borrowed time; and you can't even keep it quiet in the last chance saloon. Go on, sob out of relief, and self-reproach, aren't you used enough to it?

A lifetime of self-excuse leading to this. A life's worth of figures, waiting over your shoulder, patient for the time when they'll make the reckoning with you that you somehow slithered out of during your given time in the living. You piled them up, the victims of your behaviour, and you thought you could put it out of mind, but even this seedy little distracted conscience couldn't stem the guilt forever.

Distractions are needed, I'd say. Come on, have a drink, what else are you good for? That's the spirit, feeble skeletal hands pulling on a shirt and some trousers already. That's the engine that kept us going, that got us here. Well, when you can almost see them all gathering round, the cut-off, the violated, the ones who simply deserved love (yes, even yours, you wretch), time to keep up the blotting-out of them, isn't it? Why, you can even start to make out their faces if you stop to allow them to form. Light!

Yes, light, I've pulled open the curtains that I must have left closed. The sun is stinging less than before, must be past mid-day. Wipe the tears off that newly-washed face, why I feel as good as new. Just avoid the mirror, you know you don't. Fine. I don't want to spend a free afternoon in this bedroom that has kept the must of me. Never liked hanging round bedrooms since women gave up sharing them with me.

The bar. Yes, the bar.

Why travel far when it's right here and they call you sir, no matter what? Oh, but this is where I'm on my best behaviour, why wouldn't they.

The big bay windows facing out to sea, yes, could be one of the swanky places in Brighton or Blackpool or fuck knows where, Southend, for all I remember, from my youth. Light pouring in and nothing out there but sea, because we've reached the edge of England and it's all behind you.

It's all behind me now. No. Back to where I am, and the task in hand. A bar stool, far away from the admittedly sparse amount of guests. I'll enjoy a while unmolested, thanks. And barely a minute before a cold one is before me, that's good, the tip now is justified, it'll get me quicker service once the time is right. Uh, come to think of it, who are the people potted around the corners of this room? Few old gimmers and biddies, who are probably my age or younger. Fine. I know I will not be seen here, all the tadpoles and manatees working on the shoot will be around town. Yeah, blessed peace. For a while. Enough. Take the first gurgle.

Now, I relax. Safe under the umbrella of having nothing to do, no-one to call on me. Keep looking around, into the light space. One leg swinging off the bar stool, it's ok for now but I know the pins and needles will come soon. Flash a bit of varicose vein, see if it'll get one of these biddies interested. It'd be nice to see some interest.

But I've had my fill. I had my luck. Years of improbable luck. For everything, all horrifically undeserved. Well, being a bit known, and a bit notorious all those years, it brought interest upon me. And allowed licence for barriers to come down.

Don't think of the damage. You know well what's waiting on the ultimate tally. You've got this far scot-free, and now no-one gives a flying fuck who you are or what you did over that time. So, that's the hope. It's what's waiting after that's chilling the bone marrow. And the sign has been given. Time is gone, old stick, you're on the cliff edge. Yes. Faust quietly panicking in his study whilst the man in the gown with a brimstone pong stands in the shadows, grinning. And he looks like the young me. The one that's still leering from a screen or two somewhere in this world. And look at me here.

Focus. Other leg up now, shake it a bit, going dead, don't let that spread to the rest of you. Huh. Better, rest elbows on bar. Exhale, not audibly, no sign apart from the rattle.

It doesn't surprise me to be dying alone. Well, I'm not on a mountaintop or at the bottom of a pyramid or anything. That'd be fierce. No, lots of people, lots of activity, the miracle of final work, a moving memento mori. That no-one will see. No-one who knew you. No, no-one who cared. Or loved. You left none of them in the end. Fool. No tears, fool, you're in public.

Yes, people everywhere, but a different world, could almost be a different species. Specious connection. Like they're behind a gauze screen, sound and movement can be seen but I'm in my own little fading version. Just focus on getting it done, do what's needed and let that be an end of it. Aren't they amazed with the actual work? Yes. Yes, they are, and you know, don't you, it must be partly because they're amazed that an undead and sodden thing like you can conjure it up to order. Good grief, can't they guess that you've been doing this since their parents were scabbing their knees in playgrounds? Second nature for me alright, I've known nothing else to do for my dollar. Dinosaur. Fossil, soon.

I amaze myself with my ability to pick up and learn this made-to-order trash, this hapless guff. How does it stick in my dried up fig of a brain when the rest is fading, rapidly. So rapidly it could be fiction for all I guess nowdays. Made your living through fictions and now you can't get to the truth yourself, that it?

Or is it that you'd prefer it that way.

I think that might be it, mightn't it?

Been staring at the glass. Up, look into the light. Regard the calling of the gulls. But no elysian memory came up from down there. Sense of an edge having been reached. And all that luck having been used. In bad faith.

Everything happened to me. At the start, isn't that true? Yes, Dermot, you never sought it out. Young sportsman on trial for his team, picked up for some bloody advert or other, there it was, your face everywhere and offers, sudden offers and interest. Of many a kind.

Oh for those poor fecks who strove to get in there with no success, or who worked for years at god knows what for no thanks and probably no success. And then here's me, my leering phizzog looking down at them from hoardings and inky print, mocking them alright. Saying subliminally that this was what they had been looking for and it 'aint you. Tough gig, folks. Eat up your chips. Had paused to think back then, really thought about what was going on outside my private circus, what would the thoughts have been? No, be honest with yourself, now. Yes. Laughter. At the luck and unfairness of it all, for in this game your luck cancels out a hundred others in a decisive swipe. Well, boo hoo, I'm glad I did the right thing and didn't think about it at all. Yes, the moral option, not that I knew it.

I wonder, though, I wonder, if those candidates that fell short, say some are still around now; if they knew what's at my back, would they exchange it for living my life over? Odds on, given the same circumstances, they'd have lived the same. They would have, who wouldn't. And incurred the same.

Now if I could rewind-

-oh come on, don't get so trite on yourself. If I could go back, is that what I'm saying? No, no, every decision creates a concrete path that can't be shirked out of, we all know that, surely. Ah, but, come on, after all I've given, all the versions of myself printed off, edited, spooled out in darkened rooms, maybe some of it will have rubbed off? Rewind the film. Edit stuff out. Cut entirely.

Feverish thoughts brought about by terminal panic. You know you've lived by no guidance. Causing a whirligig of damage. And for nothing. But come on, come on, what is this that you're doing? A final spurt of luck that's been bequeathed to you from the impending void? Yes, that's of course why I care about fucking it up, even though I know I'm powerless against drowning myself despite it all. All skills I have are strictly subconscious. But it's here, you'll do it, it'll be done and you will have proven to yourself that you were worth someone's trust, faith. Doesn't matter that it's unsalvageable shite or that the director wouldn't know where to point his dick if he needed to piss let alone point a camera to get anything decent. That's just opinion, and your opinion at that, so you can put that to one side for one thing.

Just don't question the weirder factor. The one that's really knocked you for six. The fact that you're dead and some people out there know it already, it's official, just that no-one took the time to let you know.

Oh but that can't be avoided at all, really, can it? Tell me, I know I'm the only real audience left to me, tell me again so we can straighten it out, old man, how it is that you know that you're dead, damned. It's as true as concrete underfoot from where I'm sitting so let's haul over some coals. It could be that the more you look into it the more you'll find that this is some lucid nightmare that's gotten out of hand, eh? Granted, never had that happen before, but this mind does seem to be moving in ever decreasing circles.

No. I knew what I saw and I held it in my hands. When? Months ago now, half alive on the northern line for some damn reason. Gerry. I'd been to meet Gerry for our yearly chinwag. So I'd been on my best behaviour.

Every year, a meeting with the agent to see if I wanted to carry on. His little office in Kennington, neat, bright, recently I'd come to wonder how he kept it like that. No, how he kept it at all, he wasn't making any commission from me after all, and virtually everyone else on his books was having a quiet decade or two.

Every year, the same offer, I'll keep myself on the books if you're happy to pay the subs and still send me up for work, yessir, that's my contribution. Forlorn hopers, the both of us, is what I thought that day. All I could imagine happening when my photo flopped onto some big-shot baby's desk is it flying straight into the bin. Beyond notoriety by now. Swimming in obscurity. Ok, drowning.

-Each year I can see any interest you have in this business wane a little more, you know, is what I remember coming out after I'd said the usual. Yes, thought I, yes you know me well, still I came into this industry with ease so what have I to lose by someone fishing for more luck on my behalf? Bless him, in his neat little jumper, how can I say no to a man who seems to run on hope, even when pretty much every black-and white photo on his office wall is of a roundly rejected client and he must know that the game will be winding up for him at some point soon? We're rejects, Gerry, they may as well be seeing us in sepia. I may have said that. It'dve been eloquent of me. But what we did do is hug before I left. He felt chubbier every year, this one a good extra bit of bulk. I no doubt fell disconcertingly skeletal to him each time too. 'Now make sure I have the correct number for you in case I have to contact, is this it?' Ye gods that must have been a number of mine once, but I can't remember where, here's a couple of numbers to try. I gave him numbers of a couple of reliable friends who have been known to put me up in times of need. I knew they'd contact me if the improbable happened. I had, and have, no idea what my actual number is, although I do frequently have it written on a piece of paper about my person.

-No mobile phone for you, yet, I see?

-Gerry, god, come on. I'm not part of that world. Not for me.

-Well, we shall see.

-Hmn. See you next year, then, eh.

-Or sooner, who knows.

-Gerry, m'dear, your hope springs eternal.

And after a quick baleful glare from his fat spaniel, who'd been taking all of this in whilst being lodged in the corner, I was off and the day was mine. I wandered down to the open ground near the war museum, took my little travelling bottle out of my coat pocket, and gave the place a good sit. I'd be prepared to do so for a while but each year the area seemed busier, more full of the kinds of kids you see in mugshot on news bulletins. Even, dammit, in the afternoons. Just where was it safe to be an old drunk in public now? The balance of power was not in my favour, us old reprobates were at the lower end of the see-saw.

After a couple of moves away from groups that seemed to be incrementally moving toward me, I retreated to what looked like it could be a pub. It was getting dark by then. That's the odd thing about having little to do with your time, it disappears anyway; so much for the leisure time I promise myself every morning. Anyway, although it was some kind of pub I knew that hanging out in it would be a bad idea as soon as I went in, they were playing some kind of music that sounded like some drugged up eejit banging a log, and the staff looked at you like you needed something. Yes, which I did, of course, but they couldn't help.

Was that maybe something at the back of my mind, a sense after the meeting earlier of something valedictory? Was that feeling priming you to see something to confirm that feeling? Nah, I can't give credence to that, I was drifting about as usual, it's not like a had a surfeit of feelings, even at the most heightened of times, isn't that it? Anaesthetised as usual. I was drifting like a fat dog prowling for meat.

So that's where it happened. On the underground platform, doing nothing but waiting for something to take you back to your latest dive. Swaying, I'd bet, but glad that it was still afternoon and there weren't many people that I'd have to avoid. Yes, right. Muggy enough down there, the usual oppressive feeling bearing down on you, you saw that there was a few minutes before the next train. A sly slug of the whiskey, why not, it'd been a civilised afternoon. The electronic clock kept saying four minutes for more than it should, after a while you were sure you'd been there for five or more.

No great bother, nothing to do, after all. Another sup. No-one about, in fact. Creeping feeling that you'd missed out on something, were people supposed to be down here? Yes, it's just that most people aren't dossers like you and don't need to be down here at this time of day. Then.

Another breeze, not from outside but down there, warm and unwelcome, from the movements of some far off train. Stung your eyes, in fact. You wiped the rheum. Then the fluttering of an abandoned newspaper down by the tracks caught your vision when it cleared.

A sharp, aggressive face in black and white staring out right at you. Obviously from decades ago, the photo, and a nanosecond before you realised who it was.

Dermot Boyle indeed, you still had it in you to recognise yourself. Well this was a turn up. Shame that no-one is here for you to point out your self to, that's what the first thought was. Then, what the dickens can it be for? Showing an old film of yours tonight somewhere? No, you'd have heard about it from Gerry, if there was any kind of money on the way. Closer, you looked. A quarter page of text around it, can't make out the words but it's clearly you alright, an old promotional photo. Some recap of some old sordid scandal? But why, who would care? And then, no headline, nothing but a stark-

Dermot Boyle-

And-

And there's cold sweat on my temples even remembering it...but we're here to remember, aren't we. So tell us again.

'Dermot Boyle, 1935-2004. Volatile Actor of early promise'.

And by then, only just then in the hypnosis of terror did you realise the train was coming in, the wind whipped at the page, turned it in on itself and then the whole thing was lost under the carriage. Gone in blackness. Just like your old useless self, so you saw.

And yes, I had no recollection of getting back, I must have done so on the bloody train, all I know is I was looking for that page anywhere, yes, in the carriage, pavements, ripping papers out of people's hands, yes, possibly. Can I be blamed for doing so?

And then the raving down the phone to a friend or two who no doubt tried to point out, wouldn't we have said if we'd seen that you were dead and let you know, what kind of friends do you think we are, after all? Oh fat fucking laugh that is.

No. No, there was never a trace of that thing again, but of all the be-sotted years I've had, I've never had my eyes betray me. What I think is – I've seen something that's just around the corner. I've heard of people seeing similar. And I know that the wizened old fool face that the world sees here is just a convenient skin hiding a man who's done far too much wrong in his life to not be due some reckoning.

Because that's why I'm always riffing off against myself like this alone, isn't it? Oh yes, I can't even begin to have confidence in anything I experience being real at all, starting with myself.

Oh-god. Where have I been? Went in too deep there. I wasn't talking out loud, now, was I? Look around. No, the oul manatees are as quaint and quiet as ever. And you weren't crying, were you? No, no, rheumy of eye, but that's senescence. Straighten up and order another beer off that young one there, it's your day off and you'd better bury those feelings and relax the hell out of it, or you'll regret it. Yes, of course-

-Could, I–please?

Ah? Ah yes, he has pointed out that you seem to have drained your earlier one and already, at some point, ordered another, which is happily full and waiting in front of you. Now...

...when the fuck did that happen?

Where the hell have you been? Hiding? Starting to wonder if you're hanging around someone else. What's that smile for? Wish I could. What, since I last saw you? Yes, lots has happened. Everything's weird, most people have lost their shit and I have no idea how everything's carrying on, or if anything will actually finish.

This shoot is like some skewhiff engine that's gone kaput and can't function for what it was designed to do, but keeps whirring on, dripping pus and spouting steam. Yes, I'm in a state, can't you see my eyes. I'm kholed-up because they look even worse underneath.

Five screaming fights, three breakdowns, and a battered owl. That was all in the last five-four? Five. Five days. Non-stop. Most of the crew aren't talking to each other at all, let alone me. A zombie crew. I keep looking at the lighting rigs and wondering if one of them will come loose and kill half of us. That's not just because I'd quite like them to, it's because the sparks are so out of whack they don't even respond to their own names. No, I wouldn't say it's been more exciting, either. No matter how stressful a film set gets it's always repetitive and dull, it's just that they can get a psychotic overlay. Hey hey, here we are. Hope it's been better for you, wherever you were.

The owl went down on Tuesday. I've seen squabbles happen on sets, but when a barn owl gets a smack upside its 360 degree revolution-equipped head, you know you're in the seventh level of film hell. Not that it was entirely blameless, but hey, in this case it was the clear victim. Poor thing, what a horrible end to it's showbiz career.

I'll say this for being constantly stoned and virtually shackled to a member of the living dead, it puts the grinding tedium of life on set into sharp relief. I mean, being in the company of madness makes all the rest of the daily tasks positively cozy. Oh, don't get me wrong, with all that's been going on since we last spoke, I may actually be having a better time of it, for all I know. Although I do wonder if that's because I've lost my marbles.

He was onto me pretty quickly. The plan, subtle as it was, collapsed like a play-dough dildo within a day or two. Yeah, I know, big surprise. But I'm safe, as far as I can tell.

I really should feel more shame at being found out by someone who, I can sadly confirm, is constantly off his chuff to the extent that he doesn't seem to know what time or town he's in, but hey, maybe my heart wasn't in it. The first couple of days had gone alright, we actually drove him to the entrance of the hotel (a distance of half a mile from where we were shooting) and when he went in, he drifted over to his door and that was that. I waited for a while, but no. The other two were waiting in their unobtrusive little places somewhere outside. The little shitty mobile I'd been given for this occasion didn't make a sound.

What would we have done if it had? Oh look, I'll...give the low-down on that later. Take it from me, having those lumps of man-gristle lurking somewhere out there doesn't heighten a sense of safety, it makes it plummet. The second night, when I was in my room and hoping for nothing to happen so that I could give a quick think about who I've allowed myself to turn into and what the hell I'm doing with my life, the phone chirruped. A text. HE MOVIN TO THA BAR. No reference to him leaving the hotel, so must be the one in the hotel. No fuss, just move yourself so some vantage point where you can keep an eye and let them know if any funny business might happen.

I opened the door slightly. I could see the spectre shuffling just out of sight, out of the corridor. Yes, they could see that. I've reconciled myself to the fact that by being complicit in this plot I'm basically allowing myself to be spied on at some points of my day. But it's a bit of extra dough, right? No, you're right, I know it's scary.

Anyway. That night I followed him down to reception and allowed him to drift off to the bar. I sat and read one of the tourist pamphlets on the desk very intently. Y'know, even when you're trying to find those things interesting, it's impossible. Anyway, after an hour of flitting between that and my phone-my own phone - I saw his shape lurking itself out of the bar and across reception. HE IZ GOIN BACK. I know. L. GIVE IM TEN MINS DEN CHECK IZ DOOR. Sure. L.

With conversation like that, I was growing a real rapport with them. I gave it the ten minutes, then gave the tourist leaflet a rest. No sign. Gradually skulked up to the corridor, the door. No motion. But some goddam weird noses from inside, alright. "Seems fine", I texted, then went in to my room before they had a chance to text back. Well, if this is it, I can cope, I thought; give or take the sickly air of subterfuge.

I also kept in phone contact with David once it was apparent that our start was locked in for the night. For the first few days, it was the same message – Safe Now? Quest. You've got to hand it to David Quest, he likes to put his name about even when the recipient knows it. That's how it went, initially, anyway. We're in a bit more trouble now, as should be obvious –

Anyway. I'll start with the owl. Why they thought an owl would be a good idea, I don't know, I guess there's been some eye-catching ones in films recently and they wanted some kind of pet that would signify knowledge and eccentricity. Bit of a cliché, isn't it? But like many clichés, it's dependable because audiences are suckers for this kind of stuff. So Dermot's character, our bumbling paterfamilias with a heretofore undiscovered heart of gold, is found early on in the film to be shacked up with a pet owl in his little house on the coast. Yes, even after all this time of Dermot proving himself to be essentially incompatible with any human that has to work with him, our powers that be have kept fixated on the idea of sticking an owl on the end of his arm for at least two scenes and having it perched in the background for several others. At least in the latter they could have cheated and used a stuffed one –fuck it, wish they'd go the whole hog and stuff Dermot and work around him that way. I guess there's still time, there would be an army of volunteers who'd be up for the job of getting him to the right state for taxidermy. But nope, improbable as it may seem, the spiteful old relic is actually very good at playing the bumbling old codger. Where does that come from? Where can he find that person in his soul, after all there doesn't seem to be a soul to find him in. Either way, he acquitted himself better than the bird did. 'Aint showbiz cruel.

There were ripples of knackered apprehension making their way around the crew as the first owl day approached. We really thought that it would be pulled in favour of something less prone to being spooked and lacking claws and a beak – a cuttlefish or gummy ferret, perhaps. These had been suggested by a concerned first AD to both David and Hero a few days before, in their portable rumpus room. Our leaders politely received the suggestion and politely declined.

So it was that Austin arrived one morning, busy with a mouse in his cage and handled by his wrangler. The wrangler explained that Austin was a relatively old owl, and also a veteran of many screen appearances, with his latest job entailing several weeks hanging off a wizard's shoulder for some interminable bollocks being shot in Slovenia. Austin, you blank-eyed old pro, I thought, how has a star like you ended up in dreck like this? The one face-to-face look we shared – just as he was being carried to the first set up – seemed to convey this. A sense of unease at the context he'd found himself in. Well, hey, I may be projecting something onto that expression, I dunno. Like I say, blank eyes and a striking face. True film star demeanour.

Now, Dermot had been his usual self in make up that morning, which is to say that although no-one had been directly physically assaulted, had a clinician happened to fall into the make up room they would have spared no time in diagnosing him as clinically insane. This, despite being an apparent problem for anyone who wasn't already insane, wasn't the main problem on the morning's menu.

No, it had become known that our star had only just the night before let the director know that he was allergic to birds. He had, apparently, been under the misapprehension that the bird would be used in cutaways rather than, as required on this day, swooping down through an open window straight onto Dermot's tweed coat and – ah, the flourish! Picking out a dead mouse from his shirt pocket.

Our boozy old star had, apparently, not grabbed the nature of this scene because he had been focusing on the dialogue rather than the bits without words, which, this one at least didn't have. Yes, given the talky, essentially melancholy nature of the film, you could say that this little vignette was one of the main points of action. Showed the character's comfortable rapport with the animal kingdom, y'see. Oh, and there was another problem with the sequence that Ron the Camera whispered to me as I saw two more anxious continuity people run into make-up.

It was the mouse. He was phobic of mice as well. -So,' (Ron hissed), -those two are going in to make up a mock mouse for his pocket.

How? -Well, they're threading some wool over a piece of sock, and tapering it up in the right places to make it look anatomically correct. That's the easy bit, though. Austin needs to want to go for it, it's what'll get him to swoop in, otherwise he wouldn't give a toss. So to keep him interested they're also sewing in a sliver of raw meat, it'll have to go in the false mouse head.

Oh gawd. -Yes, this will be delicate, so don't expect us to start for a while yet. And It'll involve some trial and error.

Yes, I thought–trial and error. This has been what we've all been up to over the last few week, lots of trial and lots of error. And why we were faffing about with Dermot's phobias and allergies, I couldn't guess – we'd all proven to be allergic to him, with a quick phobia having developed as well. Still, we weren't in front of the camera.

It was an even more blanched than usual Dermot that emerged from his cylindrical tent that morning, bleached with what seemed to human eyes like a taut fear mixed with a readiness for aggression. Coiled up, somehow. David bade him greetings, but around the rest of us folk, the needed lurkers, there was a resultant silence. Something, even more than usual, was up with the old codger. And it hadn't been a change for the better. Aside from the grisly vision of a lunatic character actor on edge, we weren't any more edgy than we had been on the last few mornings. The false mouse had only taken two hours to get to match-fit level, and there it was, being trepidatiously lowered into a mouldy-looking tweed pocket. Austin and his handler were nearing their mark.

Did I see that bird's head revolve to meet his co-star for the first time, to take him in, get the measure of him? Well, maybe I did. Maybe I'm just primed to see drama in every moment, but, dude, I never thought I'd see an owl look askance at someone. A full 360 degree twirl (how flash, right) followed by a little double-take. Did those beady eyes widen a bit? Can they? Fuck knows, I haven't looked up if they can, but more than one crew member thought that they saw a showbiz owl grow visibly perturbed, right there and then.

As for Dermot, his eyes were on the false mouse being tucked into its resting place a few inches below his chin. Those who were wrangling the mouse did their best, the usual method we'd all developed in dealing with Dermot at close quarters. That is to say, interacting swiftly, gently, then stepping away as if from a giant humanoid buckaroo which was primed to do damage at a split second.

Come to think of it, both bird and man were getting a similar treatment from their respective handlers. Only one of them seemed up for the job, though, and it wasn't the one in the tweed suit.

After the usual preliminary tedium of the set up having to be altered several times over because of seemingly pissy reasons that could in reality actually ruin the shoot, at least two tempers were visibly building up. Feathers were ruffling up on the both of them, some literal. Austin at one point looked down below his claws, down at the worn carpet, all the morning's wild contained energy dissipated. His head occasionally tilted to take in an attendant spark or continuity bod, weariness emanating from his orange eyes. Poor bugger, barely three hours on our set and he was acting as jaded as...oh crikey yes, he was acting as jaded as Dermot usually did. What kind of soggy voodoo was coming off this useless little set, I wondered? Well, we'd see more.

Dermot was sat on the far side of the set, muttering murderously to himself. Continuity were having to keep running sorties toward his coat pocket in order to readjust the false mouse. He's been steadily worrying away at it, which of course threatened to derail the denouement of the scene entirely, if we ever got there. Surely, if you're allergic to real mice, having a stunt mouse slipped in your pocket wouldn't be that much of a woe? Especially if it's your job for the day, right? Still, I also have to guess that if it's your job to blur the boundary between what's really happening to you and what isn't, a convincing mouse is as bad as the real deal.

Austin, in his own state of worry, managed to botch what was headed to be the first take by suddenly spraying his owl bowels all over the second AD, who had been stood right behind him out of shot, his hands cupped together, silently praying for a successful shot. It was quite a look. He certainly didn't laugh. Others may have. Another re-set. Another escalation of tension poinging back and forth between the two sides of the set, increasing with every passed minute.

Finally, we were ready. The very first action of this sequence was for Dermot's character to turn around with the benevolence of ages (can you imagine) as he hears his dearly beloved feathered companion (good grief) at the open windowpane. He beckons the bird over (hah!), who swoops lovingly to the top pocket and (money shot, and yes you guessed it) finds dinner hidden in wait for him.

This was actually the most complex shot we'd tried in a very long time. We'd managed to fuck up shots of Dermot opening a door, Zephiah pulling up to a bus stop on a Lambretta, and an actual static shot of the town. So you'll forgive us, back there, cold and cramped and all desperate for our own chance to go to the loo, if we were expecting a hot load of bugger-up to rear its head.

The first camera was trained on Dermot, the second directly at the window where Austin would make his angelic entrance. Shoot both simultaneously, combine them over any other long shots of the entire process, that was the idea. What actually happened:

On cue Dermot emerges, as is his way when needed, with all the benevolence and mild eccentricity that he can't bring himself to muster off set. It is, undeniably, exactly what we need. Where does this character come from? Where is he hid?

Across the set, at the window –ah, Austin, you've somehow turned from a crabby old bird into a silky old pro, morning light reflecting off your pure white feathers, those previously saucer orange eyes now expectant and innocent. Austin, you old showbiz tart, well done.

That was the first second or so. A second of perfect stillness, still captured on film somewhere in a canister in some darkened room, somewhere. As soon as the motion started, along came the disaster.

Austin, being a bird, was able to clear the window ledge in a split second, and was already closing on the hidden, false mouse, when both man and bird spasmed violently. A ripping hiss emanated, from man or owl it was hard to make out, but as soon as the crew's eyes and ears were registering the sound and image in front of us Austin twisted and buckled like no raptor should, vulnerable, wrong, terminally so.

Y'know when I mentioned different kinds of silences earlier? A concentrated film set has its own silence, and we'd been in it. But for one or two heavy seconds, a completely different silence had all of us in its clammy hand. It's one I hope you've never known. It's that of a lot of people bound together, seeing something become deeply wrong, and being frozen, hoping that it somehow isn't happening. Before anyone breaks, realises it is real and reacts, the silence is a solid thing, binding all there together.

We were all frozen when the owl twisted away from its trajectory and flew – no, was flung, out in an arc away from Dermot and straight into an awaiting spotlight lamp, where it immediately blotted out the light and emitted a different kind of hiss. The silence had broken for a nanosecond before the smell of burning feathers filled the set.

I don't remember the next few minutes or hours in general terms. Nope, its more in dreadful impressions, snapshots, little clips of outrage and panic. The owl handler's weeping face, the general melee of absolutely everyone on set bursting into horrified action as soon as the silence was broken. David, glazed, commandeering. Dermot having disappeared. Some of the sparks bending into the lamplight with their heavy gloves, heartbreakingly delicate in their movements whilst bringing Austin out of his bright, terminal eyrie. As if it mattered to him, now.

So we'd joined that dreadful club. We'd actually witnessed a death on set. Yes, an owl, rather than a human, but flaming heck, would you want to go out in that way? And in the service of something as morbidly pointless as a bloody film? Even a good one?

I know that part of the deep panic that permeated everyone then and the hours afterward wasn't just about seeing a bird get pointlessly killed in the name of bad art, of course. It was because we knew that now we were in deep shit. David was visibly blanched. Hero was, apparently, bellowing in despair on the phone, according to those who could hear through the necessary walls. I mean, owls don't have unions as such, but you know the old credit that sometimes you can't help but see as they're rolling by at the end of a film on TV- no animals were harmed in the making of this film. Well, we'd clearly broken through that barrier. This was bad news for all concerned. No wonder even the producer and director were in a flap.

Sorry. Flap. Really didn't mean that.

Anyway, look, the next question was –where was Dermot?

Suddenly everything was frozen. Those running the production were seen intermittently and, wraithlike, said little but conveyed much terror. We were a crew adrift. Hundreds of people on hiatus in a little English seaside town, slumped around each other, wondering if the work would continue. Tell me, if you take the film away from its film crew, do they continue to be a crew? Or does a new collective noun have to apply? In this case, a slump seemed to be the appropriate term.

Accident or not, something dreadful had happened on our watch and some consequence was surely hurtling towards us. Look, I've carped about the kind of people who made up the film's crew. And I'll probably carp about them again when I remember the specific individuals, but you have to imagine, these were mostly very young people on their first or second job, working like hell, on little sleep or thanks, all because they desperately wanted to make a life in it, in this stupid bloody industry. What had they got? Weeks of drizzle and tantrums, cold sores, squit doses, ruined relationships; and a creeping sense that they were welded to a turkey, (another bird reference, sorry) for all their hard efforts. And now? A wanton act of violence from the permanently-excused curmudgeon who had caused them so much strife had very possibly nixed the whole thing. All for naught, right? All manner of organisations and unions were surely picking up on this, the calls would have been made from the wrangler as soon as it had happened. It's a dreadful thing to know that turbo-charged recompense is on the way, it's deserved, and yet you were impotent in stopping the actual thing happening.

Oh, a word. Yes, we all talked about finally firing Dermot. Hell, it's what we'd been expecting since the piss frenzy of weeks before, but it hadn't happened then. And I'm sure on a normal set he would have been at that point, and he certainly would have been by this. But of all the worried communication we heard, not a sliver came through about him. The one who did the bloody thing. No word.

So we hung around in our hotels and cafes, the beach's sand blowing through the out-of-season streets, getting in our clothes, our teeth. Zephiah was elsewhere, no-one knew. We worriedly checked our laptops, trying to get an internet connection where we could in order to see where and when the story of our avian immolation would break.

Nothing was coming through. Was some kind of dark god protecting this venture? Or, worse, were we so insignificant, such a forlorn bunch, that even this outrage wasn't being received by civilisation?

People in the town seemed to be shunning us, sensing the clammy panic that had descended. I mean, also, take the film away from the crew and soon others will realise how dull the crew is on their own terms. I caught sight of myself in a sandy mirror in one of the crew vans, and realised how gaunt I'd become. The khol had seemed to fix itself under my skin. God, I almost looked on-trend. As in, ill. I'd never fallen for that kind of fashion, I mean, look, I'm middle class, but not that middle class. No, I looked sick. Pasty under flickering neon, beyond tired, worried into illness. The look was catching on. All us suddenly left shuffling like zombies, bereft of the thing that gave us purpose, cause. And completely innocent of the deed that had caused this existential funk. Only one person was.

So, where was he?

Where was Dermot?

I soon knew.

Of course I did. It was my job, wasn't it. Not that I was sharing. But look, before I tell you that, there was the news that spread round:

-They've found a replacement. They're doing it with a dog instead.

Took me a few seconds to compute that, but it soon made sense. They'd realised their central error, the reason why the shoot had hit the skids in the first place. Dermot would soon be booted out in favour of a dog.

And it made perfect sense! Look, films get made on dafter scenarios. We'd been shooting a melancholy but profound little story about a young woman returning to her grumpy uncle-or grandfather, I can't remember. They made amends about past strife and realise how precious they are to each other, yadda yadda. You see daft shit like that getting made all the time, even if you don't have the stomach to watch it. They're out there. Well why not replace the old git with a dog? Oh, right, there's the old cliché about never working with animals or children, but considering what we'd been through this alternative seemed just fine, no-far preferable. And by the way, you may have noticed that children and animals are in lots of films out there. The little shits are all over the place, so plenty of people are working with them right now. And in that instant I would have happily stepped up to the challenge. People like them! Given what you've seen of Dermot, would you rather spend two hours staring at close ups of his rotten gob, or that of a melancholy Labrador? Exactly.

It made sense, we could have most of the dialogue in voice over, Zephiah could nail it back in a Soho recording studio in a matter of days. Yeah, we'd need to reshoot lots of what we had, but we already had lots of her that we could use and I was already thinking about some tricks I could try and suggest. Cut out the amount of dog screen time by shooting from the dog's point of view! Hell, hire someone like a well known sitcom actor to be the voice of the dog! Lots more Zephiah on screen and the dog becomes ever more charming and anthropomorphised. People might actually take to it. People might actually want to watch it!

Oh yeah, the story would need some changing, but we'd be able to panic some screenwriter into getting something up to speed in a day or two. I dunno, maybe it had been her uncle or Dad's or grandfather's dog and she'd hated it but now the uncle/dad/gramps had carked it and now she was caring for it as they only had each other to help cope with their respective loss, blah sodding blah, but you see? It's an idea with wings. Ok, wings –bad memories of the owl, I shouldn't have used the phrase.

For at least a whole minute these ideas were coursing through my knackered brain, before the particularly fish-eyed Personal Assistant that had delivered the last bit of news dropped the bomb.

-No, sorry, not to replace Dermot. To replace the owl. We're re-shooting the scene in the house tomorrow with a dog. We also have a stuffed one on standby. Sorry, everyone I've spoken to had the same reaction. The dog's replacing the owl, not Dermot.

So, as the news zapped around the bedraggled crew, hope rose and was almost instantly pissed all over. Not only that little disappointment. We'd be back on the job, alright, but as we were, albeit one owl down. The groaning reproaches could be heard all over town. How were we escaping what we deserved? How was he? Something was protecting that man. So we'd still have some time together. And, of course, I still had my commission.

So where had he been those past few days? Holed up in the hotel, getting by turns drunk and stoned as hell. Like a massive red-eyed viper in his little lair. I knew that and, unfortunately, he was now well aware of me and what I was doing.

I'll set the scene –

The first day after the owl immolation I'd slept in late. I knew nothing was going to happen that day, at the least, as I'd been told so in a terse text from David I received as the night collapsed down around us. I was glad he'd found the time to reply. Up until then I'd been carrying out my routine for a few days, making sure that the old git was in his room and replying as I silently freaked out about the invisible thugs hiding somewhere near, unseen but seeing me. Trying to behave normally whilst knowing that someone's watching your every move. The more I think about it, the more it sounds like acting to me. And I never wanted to get into that.

He'd been on no more escapades after dark, at least not outside of his room, and had been waiting for the PA types who arrived before call time to escort him to wherever the shoot had been dredging on. I'd almost felt used to the subterfuge, felt like I was getting used to it. This didn't sit well with me.

So after the disaster, knowing that we'd been knocked out for at least a day, I collapsed into my bed and stayed there with no thought of spying up on the star. Hell, he'd already disappeared and I'd asked David for info, but I couldn't get to him –hence the text. After what happened I'd hardly expected him to make it back to the hotel before being fired off somewhere else to face the music. For the first time in months, I had no schedule to drag me out of bed the next day, so I allowed myself to sleep in, with disturbed dreams that you can only guess at. It didn't stop me checking the phone in panic when I did wake, but there was nothing, no summons or news. Only after checking did I think to check the actual time. Ten to midday. The first time I'd slept more than four hours since I could remember.

Not having anything to do, I schlepped down to reception. I wanted to find some of the more amenable crew, the stocky cameramen who I'd been near at the start and bloody end of the day before. None of them would be round here, of course, I'd have to walk down to the centre of the town. If there was anything to know, I'd soon know it.

Walking through the reception, I saw a familiar dark shape slumped on a high stool at the bar, across to the far left. He was looking away from me, silhouetted against the glaring sea light that was coming through the restaurant's high windows. In front of him were two pint glasses, one full of fizzing lager, the other mostly bubbly dregs. The full drink was displaying far more signs of life than he was.

Considering what had happened the day before, I was surprised not just that he was there but that he was looking so relaxed. Well, on the wrong side of relaxed, perhaps, but he was alone, unmolested by justice. As jarring an intrusion on the surroundings as a spider falling from a shower curtain. Not too bad an image to choose, that, as I'd frozen in shock, being unable to do anything for a few fat seconds of time, apart from taking in the scene and the implication. How could he still be here? Did those running this shoot know?

I couldn't complete that train of thought, as my vision snapped and focussed on a change in the scenario in front of me. The head that had had its back turned away, showing nothing but stumpy, greasy locks, was now turned to me. Almost as if some invisible antennae had alerted him to the presence of a crewmember. I'm sure that I released an involuntary muscle spasm as the face is one that you'd have to prepare yourself to see, but here it was, having swivelled around to face me as if he'd absorbed some of Austin the owl's abilities. Those baleful, bloodshot eyes were staring at nothing but me. Fuck it, how could he have known? Maybe drunkards operate on some deeper frequency where they can tell these things, but in the moment I felt nothing but fear. His face betrayed nothing.

I ran out into the sun. By the time I'd reached the central stretch, I'd made up my mind not to let anyone know that he was still about. It would only increase the general perturbation of a bunch of people who had enough to worry through already.

So when the news of his continued employment came through, I didn't just mourn the chance of us all completing something better, but also the fact that, unless told otherwise, I'd be trying to continue my covert operation under his nose when he'd certainly clocked me at least once.

Fuck, what else was I going to do, tell them I'd been rumbled and lose the extra dough? I couldn't afford to do that by then, I'd had a tearful check of my bank balance days before and had had a call from one of my housemates saying that my bills were piling up. Not asking when I'd be back, mind, just saying that those bills were piling up.

I was locked in.

Locked in, and getting more and more uncomfortable in my little shell of lies. It had enveloped me now, and whenever I was with the rest of the crew, I could feel it hardening around me. At first it was a gloopy, membranous thing, easy to put to the back of my mind, but now it was a translucent but solid, brittle, daring the truth to come out and shatter it, breaking over me and scarring my cold, tired flesh.

Oh, people had known about the stalking job at first, of course they did, but we'd moved into a different realm now. After the owl incident no-one had mentioned it simply because they thought he wouldn't be there any more. Now I'd seen him I knew he wouldn't be going anywhere, whatever dark hold he had over the people running the joint still continued. If he was going to have been sacked he would have been by then, rather than being found basking like a boozy iguana days afterward. This much I knew, and they didn't.

I've never been a professional liar before, and it wasn't weighing well on me. Damn it, I've never been much of one for little white lies or strategic porkie in the first place. Which is, come to think of it, probably why I'm single, broke and in the career doldrums whilst my 30s are coming up behind me with a cosh. But the reason is, for some people it's physically draining to be caught in a lying situation, it weighs in the guts. Some can gobble them up, wolf them down, whatever, and it makes no differ, they get addicted to doing it. That 'aint me.

Because of my role as designated stalker people were asking if I knew what had happened to him. I couldn't tell them. Not just because I didn't want to put them into instant depression, more that I didn't want to bet on my gut feeling being correct, because I didn't want it to be so anyway. But also because until I'd heard otherwise from David or Hero, until I'd been given definite news that I could share, I had to pretend to myself that I was as ignorant of where we were as the rest of them.

That's it, Dermot, David, Hero and myself. All in a little conga line of subterfuge. Uh, sorry, that image is making me feel a little sick. But I was stuck. I'd asked the invisible powers that be in there was any news, anything I could act on or indeed pass on. All I got was a HOLD FIRM text from Hero. Nothing to go on, in other words.

The same day I got glared at my Dermot in the hotel I texted back. There was no way I could not. I wanted to let them know that I knew he was there and I would surely need to be doing something, considering what had happened a few days before.

-Saw him in the bar. Hotel. About 12pm today. Can you confirm if he is staying? L.

Nothing in return, nothing for hours, until I woke to the buzz of the phone on the bedside table.

HOLD FIRM. DO NOT SHARE. LOCKDOWN AT PRESENT. HERO.

Well, with a sign off from a name as daft as that at least I could pretend that I was being hailed as heroic. But for the moment, then, the lie would have to continue, with the following dread of knowing that when the likely truth emerged, I'd have to lie myself out of the fallout and pretend that I hadn't known anything.

But why hadn't he been seen? One or both parties must have been persuaded that keeping put in the hotel was an agreeable option. The town's small, as conspicuous lunatic as Dermot would have been seen by one of the workless crew within minutes.

Mothballed, indeed. And I was in it.

At the end of the next day, the call had gone around about the scene being reshot with the dog. No-one vocalised anything more than dire mutterings. I caught Phil the camera wandering into a chain pub near the seafront and wandered in with him. He'd obviously gone in deliberately on his own to sit and drink for a short while to recover from the extinguishment of hope, but he didn't mind seeing me waving from the bar a few minutes later. Due to my in-between nature with the rest of the crew, maybe I didn't count as real company. He spoke first when I sat down-

-So you've heard the news.

-Yes. Look, I heard when everyone else did, you know.

-Alright. I'm no criminal psychologist, but you didn't need to volunteer that information.

(Fuck. I'd sounded like I was lying when I was actually telling the truth. See what I mean about it not sitting well in my stomach?)

-No, I mean...I mentioned it because everyone knows what I was doing before that happened, having to make sure he was locked up for the night all the time. But I've been in the dark as much as anyone the last few days.

-Alright, don't worry, I can assure you that no-one really gives a toss whether you've been in any kind of loop. I can speak for everyone when I say that I can't believe the fucker's still on the call sheet.

-Guess it's him or nothing for the production company.

-And the backers, not that I have the first clue who they are. Who in turn must have pulled something out of the hat.

-You mean how we're still going?

-How nothing has got out and how we're still chugging on, yes. On a film like this I've had has-beens throw a cat or kick a dog and the thing gets out, even to the local press, then it balloons up and it's all over the shop. Plus, what happened to the wrangler? He'll be part of some union, why haven't they done something?

-You mean people have been paid off, hushed?

-I mean that something is out of kilter. A big production could get something covered up easily, y'know that. They have to, things just...happen on set if there's lots of idiots pretending to do something they're not. We aren't that big, you heard the rumours about us not making it through the second week because the money wasn't there. But here we are! Some have flounced, a bird has been snapped and set alight after turning up for work, and the complete psycho at the centre of it – who wouldn't last a day as an extra on Emmerdale with that kind of behaviour on set-is back for the duration! It's an invincible, shoot, Laura, and it shouldn't be! We're the turkey that won't die!

-Well.

I was trying to find something positive to contribute despite failing to do so since the second day of the shoot. Ah – that was it. Time.

-Well, look, how long have we got left on the schedule?

-Week and a half, tops. Although that's straight through for most of us.

-And unless he goes even more off his rocker and does something like decapitating Zephiah half way through a take, we'll surely make it to the end if it hasn't imploded already, right?

-I wish you hadn't put that image in my mind, I'm thinking he could do it now. Really.

-If I've said it, it's actually far less likely to happen.

-Optimistic. You've obviously spent too much time around him if you're even coming up with twisted ideas like that.

-We've all been around him, have we spent any time in his company?

-As far as I know, no-one has, and for their own sake, I hope no-one has to.

-We'll get to the end, then fuck it. No-one on this set need ever meet again.

-Tends to be the case.

-And until then, we can think of the pay.

-We're being paid, Laura, yes, we are.

-Great. So call time is...five, isn't it.

-That it is. Scene of the crime. Literally.

-We have time for one more here?

-A swift one. To prepare.

Being back in the little cottage the next morning was as weird as I thought it would be. It was as if the last time we had shot there had been cut, edited and altered in front of our eyes. Same scene, same people, some obvious alterations, but here's take two.

Dermot was unchanged in demeanour or behaviour, predictably. Nothing was said, nothing was alluded to by him or David. Hero was around, but not on set. More than one of us felt goosepimples spreading over their body to be there, getting ready to shoot the same scene, with nothing having been mentioned in the interim. No, nothing of substance to any of us. All had been announced through second-hand updates and the expectation that we'd be there as it was our duty to do so.

Nothing, either, said from Dermot or to him. The former, I can't say anyone expected. If someone's going to be nuts enough to do a thing like that in the first place, don't expect them to break into sanity shortly afterward and go around sharing their contrition. For the latter, look. Could you expect anyone to bring it up? Even leaving aside his lunacy, doing so would be seen as a very unprofessional act and the person would be taken as deliberately heading themselves toward the exit. Bye bye, don't expect to be called by us again. Yes, I know it's wildly contradictory to expect that of the likes of us and have an omerta for the behaviour of the lead, but look, surely you're used to how these things operate now?

All was erased, all forgotten. At least outwardly.

I think the only individual on set that was truly oblivious (leaving aside Dermot, it was impossible to tell) was the dog. He was a Labrador, a great docile barrel of a thing, with that look of mild worry that makes dogs like that so cuddly and endearing. Actually, perhaps he was worried too, if he'd heard about how the previous incumbent's tenure ended from some insider...it could have ben that he was braving it out for his day's pay and glory, who knows? But from the first take, he hit his mark and waddled over to the betweeded Dermot, who bent down (he could actually bend down! Unexpected athleticism!) and hugged him, again displaying more humanity to an animal in a fictional context than he had ever mustered to a human in any time we'd known him. The dog (I don't remember his name, never learned it – didn't want to get emotionally attached in case he suffered as grisly a fate as Austin) in turn broke away after every take, padding back to his handler but still fixing his co-star with a rueful, wary gaze. He seemed to know that he was in the presence of a dangerous man. Dermot, in turn, confined himself to the usual fish eyed staring and insolent muttering when not in take.

After several takes of this, David called for final one, for luck. As we'd all been hoping, desperately, it had not only gone successfully, but without a bloody outcome. And physicalizing our inner lack of tension, as soon as the last Cut was given, the big lab let off a guff of blinding, deafening intensity, starting like gunshot and carrying on like a Yellow Pages being slowly ripped in two.

Dermot had vanished before the last parp was an echo. I was not acknowledged or targeted. I was thankful. The rest of us laughed, gagged, and smiled and waved at the dog, who was last seen staring back into the cottage, fazed by both his own produce and the euphoric reaction to it.

-I don't know where they got him from, but I'm grateful that they did.

-And that he's made it through.

-He's one of the more civilised individuals I've had to shoot recently.

-Well there you go, the happiest we've been on this entire shoot was when one of the actors farted straight at us.

-He works well, and he works quickly. Can't have been more than one day's notice. Are you sure they can't just scratch the last month's work and make him the centre of it? I'm sure him and Zephiah will get on.

-She's worked with worse.

-Well, don't be premature about this – isn't there one more scene with him and Dermot?

-There is, but I hear they're not going to push their luck. They'll either have a point of view shot from the dog's perspective or use a stuffed one half in shot.

-Well there's a brief outbreak of sanity.

After completing some establishing shots of the cottage looking all charming an English and semi-rustic (polystyrene junk food detritus and more than one soiled nappy well out of shot, but threatening to breeze in, nonetheless. Thankfully it wasn't me that had to get a hold of them and banish them to where they belonged), we were wrapped for the day. I encountered Phil again as a taxi pulled up, ready to take some of us back down to the town and the digs. He gestured that I was welcome to be a passenger. Phil and Boz, cameramen, and a pod of continuity people that I just couldn't remember the names of.

For a while, as the taxi slid its way down the hill, we were quiet. I'd like to imagine that we were all taking in the sun setting over the bay and the light glinting off the hundreds of houses that clutched the sides of the little valley. It would have made a great shot. But then again, maybe most of us didn't want to think about work. I realised that I hadn't set up a shot in a very long time. I tried to work out how long. Years at least, and I automatically felt around in the musty attic that was my mind, to establish just how long. An automatic, unconscious gesture that I nipped in the bud, to the best of my ability. Better not to know, exactly. Think about that when all this work was done, was the best strategy. Thinking about just how long you've been away from what you want to actually do will just make it all the harder. All this.

The driver had given us a couple of minutes' respite before piping up.

-Another day's filming, then?

What the fuck else did he think we had been doing? Oh, all right, he was being rhetorical, but c'mon, do you think he'd have been overjoyed if someone had walked up to his door as he was getting in for dinner and asked, Been in that taxi again all day, eh? Doubt it. But anyway, Phil piped up, mano-a-mano-

-Yes, that's us.

-I'm sure I've seen some of you lot over the last few weeks. Not all of you.

Reckon I saw him taking in some of the more presentable continuity girls at this stage, not me of course, oh not me, and for that little thing I was thankful.

-That old bloke. One of the actors, I picked him up over a week ago.

-I think we know that one you mean.

-I hope you don't mind me saying...

-Go on...

-The leathery one, bit Irish-y or Scot, I think.

-We don't know.

-Well, what a fuckin' weirdo.

A pause. Perhaps a giggle from the continuity pod.

-Don't tell him this, again hope you don't mind.

-We don't. And we won't get a chance to share this, don't worry. Uh, do go on?

Yes. I was at least a quarter amused already, the rest was worry. Please, don't say he'd been trying to hijack a cab fighting the driver mid-ride...

-Picked him up on the beach. Looked like he'd been buried in it for a couple of days.

-Right. Over a week ago, did you say?

-Thereabouts. Said he'd been camping there, was moving to the hotel that day. Not that he had any luggage with him.

Not a sniff of reaction from us, this was simply sinking in. Despite never having seen it, in my mind's eye the spectre of Dermot emerging from the beach, pissed and covered in junk, was crystal clear. Phil spoke whilst I was still trying not to see the image:

-We certainly didn't know about that one.

-I was thinking about that after I dropped him off. Was he method acting or something? You know, like that posh bloke who puts himself in a wheelchair for months or only speaks in Portuguese if that's his role?

-Ah, well, no, from what I've been filming there hasn't been much need for going wild for a few days on a beach, not really that kind of production.

One of the continuity girls muttered something about needing to go wild on a hot beach somewhere, somewhere hot. By now the idea had occurred to me that if Dermot had been the method acting kind, we could have had a good few weeks to look back on. He was, after all, playing an avuncular eccentric rediscovering a joyful part of his soul. And he was, improbably, doing it well when needed. If only he'd been a bit more insecure about his ability to do so, he may have felt the need to behave like that to the rest of us once the cameras had stopped rolling. Whatever or whoever had, those years ago, made him so comfortable in his abilities has certainly resulted in a lot of misery being spread, at least at the stage of life we'd met him at. The taxi driver, again:

-Oh right, so he is just a bit cuckoo then, is he?

(Pause. Phil.)

-Well, look, we've got a while yet to work with the dude, so we'd better keep our opinions to ourselves.

-Ah, you're a true pro. And that's all I need to know. So what's the film about, then?

Fuck me, I could feel us all mentally straining to say anything coherent about it. I surprised myself by saying:

-Oh, it's a heart-warming thing about a man meeting his long lost daughter and realising that life is great, that kind of thing. Your town has a starring role, of course.

-When's it out?

-We don't really know, we're making the thing, others will be releasing it. Maybe.

-You sound full of enthusiasm.

-Oh...(Phil picks up again as I trail off) 'Well, we're at the end of a day's shoot, we're very enthusiastic but too tired to show it.'

'Well it seems to be heart-warming stuff, alright. I can just about see the glow from all of you.'

No-one had the energy to reply to that, but thankfully we were by then near the place we'd told him to drop us off. Phil and I reached for our wallets, for the fare. I noticed that none of the other passengers did. And not for the first time.

They scuttled away as soon as the doors were open. No trace. Phil and I said bye to the driver. Once the taxi had pulled off Phil made the universally recognised blokey sign of holding an empty beer glass and swishing the imaginary contents towards his gob, a quizzical invitation forming an arch on an eyebrow.

-Ah, no thanks, I need to collapse. Maybe if we survive tomorrow.

-Tactical thinking. Fair enough. I'll take it easy on my own for tonight. So, he's been off burying himself in the beach?

-Before my stalking duties, I'm guessing, right?

-Who knows when or how, with him. Maybe there's more than just an owl carcass hidden around this town, eh?

-Thanks. Great, thanks for that. Look, stay fresh for tomorrow. More humans involved this time. Alive, for the time being.

-I'll be on my guard, behind the equipment. Hopefully no grisly occurrences to get through.

-We can hope.

Well, I tried to say that, but I was so tired that my tongue and muscles didn't really let me. It came out as 'We cope.'

Which was, at least, basically true.

I'd just got into the reception, and was already looking out for the feared profile of Dermot, when the mobile phone I'd been given by Hero parped itself to attention in my jeans pocket. I checked it by the check in desk:

Meet DQ and I at lodgings, at 7? Please. H.

It was already half six. The question mark and please were essentially an irrelevant courtesy. I had been summonsed. Hero was renting a terraced house up at the crown of the town for the duration of the shoot. Even though he'd frequently returned to London for other business throughout the last few weeks, it had been there waiting for him whilst the rest of us huddled and tried not to enrage each other in low-level B&Bs dotted around the suburban outskirts. Whether his townhouse was paid for out of the shoot's mysterious funds or his own deep familial pockets I don't know. Rumours I'd heard that had zapped their way around the crew suggested that David the director and indeed Zephiah had also stayed there at various points, during his absences or not we couldn't be sure. It seemed that there was always a safe space available for a select few, whatever was going on elsewhere.

The place was half an hour's walk or so into town, so he'd texted bang on time, really. Although it was right back up where the taxi had driven downhill. I'd just started to unwind from the day's strain, so needed to gear my wobbling limbs up for the hike.

You'll notice that there was no hint of declining the offer, of course. That's right, no option.

A bleeding sunset was dripping its last over the roofs of the neighbourhood when I got to the top of the hill, bang on time and out of breath. I drop called Hero and the door opened for me seconds later.

They were both sat on a neat leather sofa at the far end of the living room, David sitting back down as I entered.

-Laura! You're looking well.

Which of course made me realise that I probably wasn't. Right at that moment I felt a tide of sweat making its way down my brow, headed khol-wards.

-Please, have a seat, and one of these.

One of these was a small bottle of beer, which despite my earlier denial of Phil's offer, I now had no intention of refusing. The seat was a wicker stool, straight across from the mens' sofa. Standard interview set up. I sat. They had untouched bottles in front of them, and looked relaxed even in comparison to my sweaty mess. A second or two of silence as I took a sip. Should I try to keep the dialogue open? Despite everything, nothing was coming to mind. Just as I had the word 'seagulls' on my lips David thankfully butted in with-

-Well, obviously...

It wasn't obvious what he was referring to as obvious. Where were we starting from here? There were plenty of options. Was anything actually going to be referenced at all, or were they going to ignore the last week's weirdness?

-We're obviously very glad for the help you've been able to provide since we last spoke in the van.

Alright, a positive start...

-Everyone on set knows that we've had to deal with some unexpected and frankly horrible stuff. What happened with the owl was something you couldn't have prevented, unfortunate as it was.

Damn right I couldn't! What the fuck were these drips suggesting, that I could have seen what was going on in that nanosecond and thrown myself between man and bird? Despite my state, I found noise coming out of my mouth-

-I've been tasked with keeping the man away from trouble after wrap, I wasn't there to get in the way when I was on set that day, the...

Hero now boomed over me, having taken an inaugural sip of his bottle.

-We know you couldn't, and that's why we mentioned that you couldn't. Shame.

-Yes, it's a shame, in some situation there's nothing but trust standing between people on set.

Hero looked back at David with a nod, as if his last comment (which strikes me as inaccurate and asinine even now, there is such a thing as insurance) had summed it all up perfectly, and that:

-The impetus has to be that we go on. Hurtle ourselves collectively into the maelstrom of the last days of the shoot. That's why we didn't hold any crew-wide meeting to haul over the coals. We all know what we're here for, and taking everyone away from the momentum would have made the shoot even worse. We had a short delay where some obstacles were addressed-

Again, surprising myself, the words blurted out of my mouth-

-What did you do? With the owlman, the union? I thought the story would be out somewhere, that we'd be sued, finished-

-Well... (Hero now looked to David. Despite making a cursory effort to pretend that this was a two-way conversation this direct line of enquiry. What everyone else on set had been thinking for days) had obviously surprised them.)

-Certain questions are in stasis. As you'll know, we've never had a situation flare up like it. But we were able to relay the information about what happened as soon as it did to a backer who is still looking after the facts.

My expression must have perfectly conveyed my incomprehension.

-What I mean is, someone is still in dialogue with the people who could have, no could still, break any story. They may still, but until the dialogue is resolved, they won't. Now at the least that means that barring disaster, I mean, barring any other disasters, we should be able to get the shoot done.

David picked up the conversational baton for the first time that evening.

-Of course, now, you, uh. See. That this is sensitive, a sensitive situation being handled as sensitively as our contact can. So please treat it as secret –secret and sensitive information. You know this. No-one else can.

Actually I wasn't entirely sure what I did know, but given the way the mysterious contact was being alluded to, I knew that I didn't want to be in any kind of situation where I'd have to be in any kind of dialogue with them.

I took another sip of beer.

-Well, thanks. I'm glad to have been able to keep my side of the bargain-I mean my role – successful. I guess you're wanting me to carry on for the duration?

Hero now:

-Absolutely. If anything, we'll need a bit more scrutiny.

Scrutiny being the last thing I wanted to undertake on that man. I had to let them know.

-Well, there's a problem. He's on to me.

-He's coming on to you?

-No! (oh god, the thought. At least we'd been spared that side of things. Or at least I had. I knew of nothing more, wouldn't I have heard?) No, I mean that he knows I'm there in the hotel. When no-one else from the crew is. If he hasn't guessed why, he will soon. The secrecy's out the window.

-There's no guarantee that he knows you from the shoot, even if he's seen you there.

-Yes, he might not associate you with the shoot at all.

(Thanks for the ego death there, David, am I now an official invisible member of crew to the principals?)

-What I mean is, as you will have seen he's so focussed on whatever he's shooting on that day everything is a blur.

Everything may have been a blur for different reasons, but I didn't pick up on that.

-Alright, but what if he does click?

A pause, here. A faint hope that they could realise that an acknowledged spy is an essentially useless one, and that I'd be relieved of my duty, sod the extra money...

-Might not be a disaster, all in all.

-Could actually help us out a bit more.

Oh Christ. Their concept of espionage had probably been moulded by too much adolescent viewing of James Bond. Young men and film, eh?

-Sorry, I don't follow (that's it! Be honest about how confused you are, the thicker you look, the less they'll trust you).

- Well, look, I can't provide a locked-down answer for you right here. But perhaps you can turn your disadvantage to your advantage.

Now I didn't have to feign being dumbfounded. I noticed that David was staring down at his left shoe.

-I'm not sure what's being suggested, or if anything is...surely if he finds out I'm there to relay info back to you, there's nothing to turn to my, or our advantage?

-Laura, you should never have to ask for help when it comes to your innate skills. You've been able to turn around lots of awkward situations on our shoots to all our advantage, remember that's why we're asking you to do it.

Oh, right, of course, this as a new chance to prove myself and get more rewarding stuff thrown my way. I'd been hoping that they'd forgotten about that. But they hadn't, so did that mean that it wasn't a pretence? I leaned back and took in the both of them.

-So we still have our security apes outside?

-We do. They've been here all the time.

I still didn't know if I felt more or less safe at the news.

-I'd better mention this. Am I still on double pay?

-You are. Double until we're all quits. No need to worry about that.

-And, even with that, if I gave up this task, and allowed someone else, some other crewmember to take it on, for the rest of however long we'll be shooting here?

-Well you would be quitting something, I guess –

-Alright. Allrightallrightallright. I took a sip of the beer I'd barely touched.

-Alright. Said again, like most times used, simply to cut the conversation to a temporary halt, rather than wanting to close it down entirely. As I put the bottle down I realised that the onus was on me to continue. At least it wasn't so one-sided anymore.

- I, uh, I don't want to make it sound like it's the money I'm thinking of.

- Although you did mention it. So you must have thought about it somewhat.

-Yes, I did mention it because I thought of it –

-Yeah, I mean you can't mention something without thinking about it to some extent, otherwise you wouldn't be able to mention it at all.

I piped up, to shut him up.

-I mentioned it to underline the fact that, between us, the expectation is that I'm continuing in the role, for as long as needed, even though he knows well that I'm keeping an eye on him in some capacity.

Yes. Look, this may have been his first feature for a while-

(since before you were born, I thought, and not far off when I was)

-but he has decades of experience. He'll probably have known of these kind of things happening, even if it wasn't necessarily him it was happening to.

David piped up:

-It's been a standard thing sometimes, when someone needs to be there for the duration of the shoot but there's a possibility of them...accidentally...cutting loose a bit too often.

-And it wasn't the job of some underling, you understand. It's always been the role of someone from the core of the production. Anyone from somewhere else –the floor crew or something along those lines, y'know they could fall under the star's influence and end up subverting the entire job, falling into their orbit and making things far worse.

-It happened.

-There's a notorious story about someone getting drunk with Hurt and ending up in Zurich for a week. The shoot was delayed for a month whilst they tried to find them. Him.

-I want you to know that we thought of you in the first place because we trust you. We made the decision to use this tactic because we had to, and we had to make it work.

-You know as well as I do that a lot of the people on this shoot are first timers. They're good, but you can tell that they're very new at the job. Can't you? That's why it's so unfortunate they they're sharing a set with Mr Boyle on their first professional experience. We can tell it's having a bad impact on them. You see, it's....

- It's too perilous. Too have...come this far and then have things foul up. This will be finished, we'll get it in the can. If we approach it will steel. Dermot had to stay, there was no option on that. We'd shot so much and...

-And it's useless to go back in these circumstances.

- It's an issue of momentum. But, look, of all the people working on this set, you're one of the few who have worked with us a few times over. Who else is there?

God, you know in the moment I couldn't think of anyone. There was a few that had, now that I look back, but I couldn't think straight at the time. Phil, for one, had started with the company one shoot before me, but had dipped out to film second unit at Pinewood once or twice. For some reason I didn't think of him in the thick syrup of that moment.

Of course it was me! Me, the oldest and most trusted person that they knew in the whole shitty sand-blasted town. Looking back from where I am now, I'm sure that

that's how they wanted me to think. Whether this was clinically decided or had been brought about by collective, subconscious cunning, I'll ever know. But imagining myself back in that flat, pissed off and at the end of my senses yet automatically eager to say, do, think the right thing; I feel compassion. No. No I don't, I feel anger for my younger self over any lower pity.

Used. Deliberately used to do an outright dangerous job because these overgrown boys knew I'd take it out of fear of the alternative, fear of losing out on some vague promise of advancement. And even though I can remember how I was, my sluggish thoughts see-sawing between the alternatives of accepting or declining, and how agonised I was about what to do, what the best thing to do for myself would be, I pity the person I was then. Because even at that time I had a growing mire of regret building at the back of my mind. The sense that years had gone by since I'd been some bright-eyed thing with an aura of possibilities around me.

In that moment I was conscious not only that that had gone, irreversibly gone, but also that the road I'd chosen had brought me right to that ridiculous moment, being given a fait accompli by two ridiculous child-men who had somehow gained more than I knew I'd ever have. It was also impossible to turn back and get back to that point of anything seemingly being possible, it was like some mad manky jumper I'd sewn myself into. For the first time in my life I was acutely conscious of time and potential having gone, irreversibly. It gave me a sense of vertigo.

I'd devoted all my energies to nothing apart from my own ambition, and the result had been an increasingly embittered, lonely idiot cut off from the ordinary joys and consolations available to those who hadn't put themselves at the centre of their own universe. Not even the gift of friendship. The kohl and make up wasn't accentuating anything in my outward appearance, instead it was being used to cover a sallow, panicked wreck.

Still, at least I had the moments of farce to keep me horribly interested. Here's Hero, being utterly sincere:

-We do need a decision. Take your time, please take all the time that you need, but we do need you to make a decision. Soon, preferably. Pretty much now.

- As we said, it means that we're trusting you more than most. That's worth repeating. And we're paying you twice, which is twice more than some.

Then a definite pause. I realised it was such when a crackle of tension passed between them, the first I'd noticed in years. They glassily stared at each other. I piped up.

-More than some...here?

A tacit realisation between the two that they couldn't paper over this crack. Hero spoke, David gazed forward, not directly at me but over my head.

-Because of the fact that so many people want to work in this industry, it's sometimes hard for them to get a foothold on their own. It's the fateful old equation, you can get work if you have experience, but you can't get any experience if you don't have any work to show people. Over the last year we've had more letters from people in their early twenties who want to work with us to get an 'in' on the industry than we had in all the years we were producing beforehand.

David was back in the room, it seemed. As if by automatic response he said –

-People just like you were when we started working together.

- Now as you can guess it'd be impossible for us to take on all these people whilst allocating budget to pay for them in full. But we don't want to turn people away. We can't say yes to all, it's not an opportunity that we can dish out to everyone who asks, but part of our ethos – as you know – is to get new talent into the industry and support it whilst creating our own output. Of course if we took on even a small amount it would reduce the budget of what we can shoot drastically. So this time round, we've offered shoot-long internships.

- You mean, you've saved on the budget spend by using inexperienced, unpaid labour?

-Well, that's a negative spin. They aren't inexperienced at the actual work, we've picked people who excelled in their training. And as you can tell, there's no problem with the stuff they're actually doing.

-Sorry, this is still sinking in. They've been here all these weeks, getting through all this stop-start crap, with no pay coming in whatsoever?

-They may have other means, we don't really get involved in that.

I thought back to all the well-fed, well-bred types. Yes, it made sense.

-The experience that they get on this will stand them in good stead for anything they do in the future, no, actually it will ensure that they'll get work in the future.

- I've already heard from one girl in continuity who's been offered work.

-In favour of this?

-No, afterward. Well, actually, I'll need to check on that.

-And of all the backers you've managed to cobble together to make this shoot happen, I presume they'd be delighted to know that half of the crew or more are making the film gratis?

-They do know. And have known from the outset. That's the honest, blunt truth.

I didn't expect that. Hero continued:

- It's been set from the start of when we were assembling all involved – from ourselves, to the writers, to even yourself – that from whatever we were able to raise, certain amounts had to be earmarked for certain budgetary responsibilities, no question. So at a certain point we knew we could make this happen. By approaching things in this way.

A beer-sodden penny had dropped, somewhere in my mind.

-Right, so someone out there is bankrolling this purely on the basis of it involving -you? Zephiah? A rich relative of hers, right? No?

-No.

-Oh well fuck me. It's him, then, isn't it? This whole thing's in Dermot lockdown because a backer has stipulated that it's him or nothing. Well, I knew there were rich, perverse people out there but this takes the biscuit and pukes all over it. And the crew are expendable, essentially, right?

-Of course not.

-But if a few do bow out, you have a willing supply of keen, green, young types who'll fight over the chance to step into their place, eh?

-That was never the intention.

-But it was certainly the practice.

-Well. When we started this shoot we didn't have any sense of how things would pan out. If things have happened like you say, it was certainly never our intention. Never planned.

-But convenient when it did.

-You have to make the best of the circumstances that you find yourself in, as you well know. And it isn't just people involved in the finance of this who are responsible for his being here. It's absolutely true what we said previously, we've got weeks worth of great work locked down for this. If it stopped, we wouldn't be able to re-start again from the beginning. We're coming up to the far lap, the last one. Now it's all or nothing.

David picked up the baton.

-That's why we've shared this with you. No point in not letting you into the whole picture at this stage.

-So we're glad that you've taken this decision. It'll stand the production in good stead, and it'll stand you in good stead too.

By this point I remember my head drifting down to my cupped hands, heavy with blood and bad thoughts. I wasn't aware of having committed myself to anything. Verbally or tacitly. But I had no energy to fight or contradict or share what I thought. Because I didn't know what I thought. And was too stunned to try and formulate anything.

I must have said yes.

-

The next solid memory I have is of a huge, empurpled chef screaming in my face whilst a fire alarm went off. He was loud enough to make it a distracting background noise.

-They've pissed in the dinner! All of it! Every course!

-Who? The dogs?

-All of them! The dogs and the men!

I should give you a bit more context, here. A couple of days had passed by then, with various events, but this is the one that my mind skips to. This was when things came seriously adrift. The time which I still can't give credence to as real, rather than some fevered dream.

-I thought it was just the Labradors that were loose?

-Yes, the fuckin' Labradors are. But the old man and the tramps! They're in here as well.

-Well why are you shouting at me?

-You're in charge of them, aren't you?

Well. One of them, yes. Kind of. Which made me responsible for the rest by implication.

It was in the hotel. I was being shouted at in some arterial corridor leading off from the hotel's huge kitchen. Until a few minutes beforehand the room had been full of sweaty staff preparing the evening's a la carte delights. I'd been trying to locate Dermot without success for a while, although I'd been doing so near the day's shoot, on some polite little bench looking over the town. The scene had gone well, it was a few minutes' worth of heart-warming talk between father and daughter. It had been a success, which made the chaos of now, mere hours afterward, all the more sickening.

Now, you'll think me daft to have been hunting around the town when Dermot had vanished en route after wrap, but we were near several pubs and no evidence in my previous day's hunting pointed toward him wanting to go back to the hotel when he'd have so many places to hide. Indeed, I'd had to stalk him out in a place like that the day before, there was no track record of him searching out anything other than dives. He would come back to the hotel when seen and stay in, that was it.

So when I got a text from David whilst I stuck my head in the third bar in a row, saying that he was already at the hotel – and with company – I thought that there must have been a case of mistaken identity. Perhaps some fancy dress stag do had lost a zombie and it was staying there, who knows.

But no, it seems that he'd turned up near the seafront with preternatural ease almost ten minutes after we'd wrapped. By teleportation, presumably, as it would take most of us a longer time to walk. Not too far fetched, that, as apart from hitting his mark during scenes I and many others didn't really see him move of his own accord at all.

Anyway, there he was, at reception and already being assailed by a small crew of men who looked, if anything, even more dishevelled and crazed than he did. A man of certain talents, he'd somehow managed to attract a crowd of miscreants in a matter of minutes and alienated them as much as he'd done to us over the course of weeks.

Now. As you can guess, my natural instinct was to stay where I was and let nature take its course, a man like Dermot was bound to be punched to death at some stage, and I had no inclination to get in the way of any zombified fists heading his way. But I was employed to deal with this kind of circumstance, so I sprung into action mode. That's the world of work, I guess.

Unfortunately, I didn't have a clue as to what I'd have to do in this kind of circumstance. Well? What?

I was there to make sure that he didn't get into trouble, now that he seemed to be right in some I wasn't sure how I'd get him out of it. Either way, I had to be seen to be doing something so I hitched with some crew who were driving down straight to the hotel. There was no sign of Hero or David, naturally. We arrived within minutes and were greeted with the sickening sight of something definitely being wrong.

Guests were already milling about near the entrance, asking staff what was going on. The staff, in turn, were looking perplexed back at them; this was obviously something they weren't used to. Which, considering what transpired, was a good thing.

As we got out of the people-carrier we heard fearsome noises emanating from within, and more guests hurrying out, followed out by staff who looked in no rush to return. Most of those on the pavement were old and looking like a day of tranquillity had been irreversibly soiled.

Within seconds the bar manager was staring at me, expecting me to have a solution.

-Alright, so it's your man.

-Right, and?

-And he's brought all the tramps I've ever seen in this town. Into the hotel.

-Right.

-Well what are you going to do?

Now, these moments, when they occur, they can't really be reacted to with any kind of composure or eloquence. I remember blurting out.

-Ah...great! I'll have a look-

...before turning around and trying to make sure that all the other people who had come down- Phil, two continuity girls and a weeping Swede – would come on with me.

They were utterly still.

-Oh fucking come on, please.

I heard barking. Why could I hear barking?

Phil piped up.

-Hang on, now, all this was your job, not us?

-Well it was my job to keep him out of trouble.

-Right.

-Well this is trouble, now, and it isn't a one-person job.

There are so many various scenarios in life where hatred can crystallise. So may opportunities to be disappointed to the level of misanthropy. I thought I'd experienced a few in my sheltered little life by then. Not so.

When I saw the utterly inert stance of those people, who must have seen the pleading need in my eye, I knew that I'd had my first taste of the real stuff. I had to run in to the hotel just to break away from it, or I'd have snapped and attacked them.

Seconds later a young chef was running toward me, pursued by an excited, fat hound; which hovered above the ground just behind him like a hairy torpedo. Within two seconds I saw two wildly different expressions in both pairs of eyes: the chef's a mixture of fury and panic, the dog a depthless joy. The human clocked sight of me. In the nanosecond it took to register and recognise me he caught himself on a wall-mounted fire hydrant and banged down to floor level, the dog elegantly torpedoing over him. Seconds after the dog had passed me the man looked back up at me, embarrassment mixed with cold fury:

-You!

-Me?

-Have you come here for him?

Here we go. Time to find out the worst, how this happened.

-Who do you mean?" I wailed pointlessly.

-Him! The man with the old face, the one you're with here. He's brought all of them here.

-The dogs?

-The dogs and the angry tramps. He came back and they all rushed in. Why did he have to make them all so angry?

I heard the unmistakable wailing of a fat man coming from behind the wall.

-He does that. To everyone. Including me. And you, now. I don't know why, and I don't know if it's deliberate.

-He's a cunt.

-And you've only just realised? How long has he been here?

-Stop talking and do something, you're his minder!

-I'm not his fu-

But ah, yes. I was.

Before I could make the confession, the wailing had grown closer. We both tried to concentrate on looking as if we knew what we should be doing, and before then a fag end of a man turned around the corner, continually wailing. What I initially thought was an old man was, in fact, a life-ruined wretch of indeterminate age. All was mottled – skin, hair, indistinct clothes. All apart from his eyes: primary blue irises surrounded by red, and streaming tears which ran in rivulets down his gashed and craggy face; in turn breaking down clumps of sand that clung to his face like a personal, parasitic beach.

Both his hands were trapped in a large object which, whilst trying to get himself out of, swung like a club before him. After half a swing I realised that he'd somehow become trapped in huge, glistening and irreversibly spoiled roast chicken.

I still mourn for that bird today. Thankfully chef made a lunge for the fusion of man and bird before I had to think about taking any action, and soon both were on the carpet. I'd thought that Mr Chef was trying to extract what could be salvaged of the bird from the wailing man, but soon realised with-I'll admit -utter fascination, that he was instead using it as a weapon to pummel the poor man with.

I must have stood and taken the sight in for a few minutes or so, partly due to fascination, partly just because I had no previous experience of what to do when faced with a physical altercation involving a roast bird, a chef, and a hobo. Maybe I should be saying that I'm ashamed I did so, but no; that'd be a complete lie. I was glad to have been there to see it: the glazed bird body repeatedly smashing into the tramp's already ruined face; his tears and snot mixing together to make a mulch on the plush hotel carpet. The man's attempts to sob being repeatedly cut off as the chef swung the dead bird back again and again, momentum building as in turn did his anger, the wretch's whinnying being increasingly drowned out by the guttural fury of the chef's utterances, somewhere just outside of language.

Maybe I should have felt bad for being so fascinated. Maybe I should have tried to help in some may. Oh come on, who am I kidding? There was nothing that I could have done. And anyway, I'd gotten to be where I was by being one of life's natural watchers. It wasn't, isn't, in my nature to try and budge my way in and alter things that are going on. Well, not when they're interesting left as they are, anyway.

The only thing that stopped me from gawping, in fact, was the sight of the main instigator himself. To my dread, I saw the spindly figure emerge from the smoke like a wraith. A staggering wraith, carrying a frozen dog.

Yes, the dog was a fairly large Labrador shape, and frozen. He must've done something unspeakable with it in a walk-in freezer for it to have become so stiff-legs jutting out to attention even as he struggled to carry its dead weight. The head was fixed and serene, its eyes open and glassy.

God no, I thought. Not another animal fatality. No breath was coming from the frosty muzzle. Just let him cark it this time, I thought, as he surveyed the evidence of his actions. Let the dog be defrosted, somehow, but let this wrecker of a man go to where he needs to, so he can atone for whatever wrong he'd got up to over god knows how many decades. Freezing a poor dog to death. Just how much grotesque damage could someone get up to whilst trying to film a heart warming piece of shit about the importance of family?

Dermot's expression was, whilst I thought this, looking like a beatific boy that had found all his favourite toys piled together for him. It was the happiest I'd seen him. No, it was the only time until then that I'd seen him express anything discernibly positive. He looked like a leering man-in-the moon, like the one I'd seen in an old French silent film.

Grotesque.

I did what any sane person would, even though I wasn't sure if I still qualified as sane after the last few weeks.

I turned and ran. It came easy to me. Frankly I'd been wanting to run for a long time now, run from everyone surrounding me, the crew, the locals, everyone. Something had been building, every day brought a feeling of drifting away from what I thought I should have been doing with my life. I'd sacrificed and scrabbled my way to this place, spent most of my twenties focusing on getting into this work, and I'd been so focussed that I hadn't realised what was actually happening. Plummeting into pointlessville. Dealing with idiots and a running after a madman. Never having felt less safe in my life, only then did I admit to myself that no-one running the circus cared for my safety.

So if it was a dereliction of duty, it was a duty I'd never really asked for, coerced rather than volunteered. And when you're trapped in circumstances that demand nothing but adherence, sometimes the only response is to run. Dermot and his dead dog both turned to face me as I skidded by them, the sound of the pummelling chicken receding as more male voices rose up in the corridor behind me. They added another layer of aggression that I needed to run from. No more madmen for me. I clocked a jolt of panic in Dermot as I passed, boyish joy evaporating as he registered the men behind me.

-The seals of death!

Whatever that meant.

-Laura!

He knew my name. That almost made me stop, it send a fresh wave of fear through me. He must have seen me before, but he knew me? This was a new level of creepiness – how much had he know of what I'd been put up to, who I was? Had he been keeping tabs on me as much as I'd been compelled to do on him?

I realised that I'd stopped. I was looking back, and in disbelief. He, in turn, was glancing over at me whilst looking the growing horde of battered men shuffling down the corridor. They were displaying a group intent, and it was definitely directed toward Dermot. But for the two men rolling on the floor, bound to the glazed bird, they would have already made contact. Dermot in turn was still struggling with the stiff dog, weighed down but unwilling to let go of it.

-Help!

That should have been my first impulse, to help the star, who was undeniably in deep shit. But I was divesting myself of that duty. At a rate of miles per hour. I turned again and ran straight out.

In the short time I'd been inside the hotel a large amount of the crew had gathered outside. Sirens and screeching tyres promised the attendance of emergency services. Good, I thought, it'll be their job to sort this out. And perhaps they can save me from this shoot, if I sit one or two people down and tell them what we've been up to.

I stopped once I was clear of the hotel and dropped to my haunches. I was more tired than I should have been – had I even eaten since daybreak? The members of the crew that were there looked pallid, stunned. They all saw me. No-one came. No-one apart from Hero, who was striding up from a land rover just as I was collapsing. Just the man I didn't want to see. Bad timing on my behalf. He came straight to me.

-Is he in there?

-I'm fine.

Something had truly snapped. I wouldn't have replied like that before, although I was still compelled to fill the aghast second of silence with-

-Yes, he's there.

-Then why are you here?

-It's kicking off. What do you want me to do? There's a load of aggressive old men, what's a girl going to do?

Other than have something dreadful happen to her.

-Well at least bring him out...

-Can't he do that himself?

I thought of Dermot affixed to the stiff dog. Perhaps not.

-I'm not going back. Look! I was employed to keep him out of trouble. He's in trouble. So, too late! And if you want to fire me, fine. It seems to have all happened in about ten minutes.

-I can't fire you, who else would I be able to get in?

I didn't know how to respond to that, I just let it sink in and slumped further.

-Look, the police or whoever can sort out the overall situation but if we lost Dermot the whole shoot's fucked. Maybe just open a door and see if he can jump out, or something? I have no intention of putting you in harm's way.

-If I'm going anywhere near that, you're coming too.

-I can't go in there, I'm the producer!

When I tell you that I did end up turning around, I think you can understand that I was doing so more to get away from him rather than to get back to whatever was happening in the hotel. Stuck between two magnetised poles of male idiocy. Getting away from both was the only option I wanted to take, and it wasn't on the menu at the time.

The police hadn't arrived by the time I was back inside, but I could hear the sirens approaching, they were melding in with the oddly high-pitched shouting of the enraged vagrants who were now tearing into the hotel and each other. Dermot and his dog were nowhere to be seen. Such high wailing – why, I wondered as I skidded around them – had years of exposure to the salty wind out there permanently frozen their bollocks? Was there anything left of them? I held tight to one of the fire doors, far enough way from them so that if they clocked me and came my way I had enough opportunity to run. No Dermot in sight, but plenty of carnage. Various stains now decorated the walls and ceiling, a ladle spewing lumpy brown liquid flew out from the crowd and smashed a light into skitters, dropping to the carpet a few feet away from me. Something similar was dripping from one of the doorframes. Ominously, there was no sign of either of the men who has been attached to the roast chicken, although, I guessed, they could have rolled off down another corridor and carried on the fight out of my eyeshot.

But no sign of the reason for all of this happening. The men filling the corridor were focussed on something, but it wasn't human; something had been taken from the kitchen and was being snapped apart and distributed around. One of them was wearing a chef's hat-incongruous enough on a chef but grotesquely so here. As yet, none of them had expressed any interest in me, or indeed acknowledgement of my existence, which was a relief, but I knew that this state couldn't last. Unless they'd completely vapourised Dermot (not such a bad scenario) he was somewhere else in the building, although if he had managed to give these people the slip he'd presumably dumped the dead dog by this point.

I backed away whilst they were still essentially oblivious to my presence. Over the last few weeks I'd gotten used enough to the hotel's layout to know that the door to my left led to the reception, even if I wasn't going to find my quarry (and I still wasn't sure that I did) at least if I could get there I'd be closer to any police or the like, and presumably a smidgen safer.

Passing through the empty corridor I heard some dreadful sobbing raising out of a room to my left. The door was open onto some unwelcoming darkness and a large lump that was emitting the sobs. Jesus. What the hell had been happening here? Something swift, brutal and unpleasant, more than I'd guessed at. But in that moment I didn't investigate the room. I just wanted to pass by, and anyway I was sure that the sound wasn't emitting from Dermot, although I couldn't be certain that it hadn't been caused by him.

The sirens had grown closer, and I could now hear police coming into the building, shouts of reply already coming from the assorted tramps. No cry from Dermot, though. Instead I heard a piping quack from an antiquated car horn – nothing contemporary, but something shrill, comedic, as if Mr Toad was announcing his arrival, or if a clown had fallen over.

Right then Dermot came into view. He was on all fours, shielding himself from the increasing throng with the frozen Labrador. By then the wails of the tramps were growing closer, they'd be in the room in seconds. Some police were already clomping through the main door. This was Dermot's cue to move. But first –

-Fine fuckin' help you were, eh?

-Well I'm here, aren't I?

He didn't reply to that, but instead placed the dog flat on the polished floor and shoved it. It slid across and he went with it, in the direction of the bar-as ever. I would never have put money on the sight of a decrepit actor using a stiff dog as an improvised vehicle being something that would escape a policemen's attention, but the two that were now in the room had been distracted by the crowd of homeless men, who were increasingly agitated. Perhaps, I wonder now, at the thought of their intended prey eluding them.

Even in that state I knew what Dermot was up to. Or, at least, if instinct was dragging him in the direction of the bar, it was serving him well. There was a fire escape at the far end of the bar, and although it would likely be covered soon, the cops' current focus meant that it was almost certainly free. I backed away from the crowd and entered the bar, just in time to see Dermot attempting to wrench the Labrador out of the fire door.

-Still here?

-I don't have a choice. What the fuck is all this? What did you do?

-Fucked if I know.

The comedy horn sounded again – closer to where were, this time. By then I knew that Dermot had a definite escape route. He had finally manged to lift the blocky dog and was balancing himself out of the door.

-What's with the dog?

-I like him. I'm looking after him.

The horn sounded again.

-God damn that bloody thing.

He said this whilst almost collapsing through the door, by the time he was out I'd made it to the door myself. He was walking as quickly as he could to a car that looked as battered and forlorn as himself. Stood by was an odd little man in bottleneck glasses, who was waving his right hand whilst holding the horn in the other. He gave it a final, redundant parp.

-Leave the horn out, will ya? Stop drawing attention to us.

-You're a professional actor, you old tart, I thought attention was what you wanted?

The man's voice was plummy, like something from those English literary adaptations that I never managed to watch the entirety of.

-Context, Roy, context. Help me with this dog, will ya?

-Handsome beast. What's his name?

-Fuck you, is his name. We'll decide later-come on.

-Fair enough. And who's she?

I had been so perplexed by this little vignette that I hadn't tried to either conceal myself, or make any attempt to apprehend Dermot.

-That's Laura. She was part of the crew.

-Was?

-As was I. Now help me get the hound in the back, will you? You can sit beside him.

The last few seconds had allowed me to take in the dog's blank gaze further. I could see that although there wasn't any life in the thing, its time had ended far further back than I feared. Rather than being frozen, the thing was taxidermized. It had also worked on the set, as the stuffed replacement for the day-playing Labrador. One of the more reliable fixtures on set, essentially kidnapped. Now I was helping Dermot himself shove it into the back seat of some saggy disgrace of a car. And I was following.

As the car rattled out of the hotel car park I could still hear sounds of commotion. People were still in some state of strife, but I'd had enough. I knew, crazed as my choice was, that staying there, in that context would only result in my being part of it, being implicated. Better stick with the stuffed dog and the psychopath.

And a blind man, judging by the dangerous lurching that we were going through as the car banged its way into the road. I was trapped under the Labrador and couldn't see the traffic, but I could hear the parping and tooting of various horns, some flying close to the car itself. Why wasn't I panicking?

-Fuckin' hell Roy, have you got your eyes on the road at all?

-Very sorry, um-

The plummy man seemed to be sniffing at the air in search of the right route-

-I've not got the right ones on.

-What? What? What do you mean?

-Don't have my right glasses. These are my reading glasses.

-Oh Christ.

-Sorry, I was in a rush, after all.

Something blasted past us on the outside lane, swearing.

-Try to have a little faith.

After being in motion for so long, I allowed myself to freeze. Quite what I was doing in the car, I wasn't sure, but I was aware that I'd severed any chance of not being in a very dire problem indeed with my paymasters.

I squeezed my right hand down to my right jeans pocket. The phone was stuck in there, bringing it out hurt my cold knuckles.

I made sure that it was off.

The stuffed dog 's front legs were wedged across my front, paws stuck at the door, the whole thing acting like an hairy crash barrier. The dead hairs were bristly and damp. Nonetheless, I allowed my head to slump and connect to its snout.

'Get your head off that dog. Have some respect, can't you?'

After that I must have fallen asleep, or passed out...

Now. Must be seeing things, my eyes are open. What? Musty room. Stationary. Weight on my lap, what is it? Bottle of something, something mostly drained. Pain still there, behind the eyes? Yes, yes and more so. Good. Good to see you're still about, old pain, and thriving. Thanks to your own connivance.

Musty, dark room, figure on a sofa. Wheezing. Ah, Roy, it's you and this is your place, back again. Yes, you drove me back, I remember parts of it, a familiar face and lots of commotion. But from what -? No.

No, leave that till later to think about. Concentrate on being here for the moment. I'm definitely in pain, so I'm definitely alive. You'd think. Still, no point of comparison with the other option, but I do seem to still be respirating. Cold sweat. And I've woken in a red leather chair. Very regal. There he is, still wheezing that round belly of his out and back, he'll probably take a good hour or two to wake up. And that gives me time for another glug or two. I can feel a bit of something sloshing about in the bottle and I do believe he's left a sizeable glass of red over on the side table. Rich pickings, if I can get over there to pick it up without waking him I'll deserve it for breakfast. First challenge of the day, and I'll gladly take it up. Bottle of whatever this is back down on the chair, smoothly, that's right. No sound. Ah! A creak. Of course, the bare floorboards, it's how he likes it here. Probably kept it this way over the years so he'll hear if someone's trying to pinch some of his booze. Well let's see if your plan worked, you mad old ham. No, wait, pain in a different place. Between the brain and the floor. My knee. One of them, this, the left, that was the creak, and yes a fair bit of pain. Don't let that stop you, Dermot, just rest your weight on the other leg, it's still there, don't let a crumbling kneecap stop you.

Ah jeez, right over the fireplace, we were talking about it last night at some juncture. The photo, Roy's finest hour. Resplendent, at the peak of his career, not that he knew it at the time. He obviously likes to keep it there to remind him of when it was all going well. Isn't that a daily curse, then, to see that and be reminded that it's all over? Perhaps I was saying that last night. Christ I hope I wasn't rude. Of course I was, I'm sure. Taken in the early seventies, must be, next to the star of the show, couldn't remember his name last night so I'm not trying now. Frilly shirt and velvet jacket. Publicity shot, Roy looming at him with as much threat as he could muster. Less recognisable, what with being under all that green latex, of course. Now when I say less, well not at all really, as it's not even that he's wearing a mask, it's his entire head that's covered by an all-enveloping bulbous appendage with two fishy eyes plopped on the top and, I must note again, pointing in two utterly different directions. The effect is more than slightly comical, but this is it, Roy's shrine of When. Bless you, ever the trier. Ever the failer. You must have been insanely jealous of me at some points, surely. During all my gallavanting and success. Everything happened to me, and nothing much to you. And for all your trying. Now did I ever even tell you the worst part, I wonder? At some point back there, I wasn't even trying. Others did it for me. I would have been jealous of me, had I still given a tuppeny fuck about the whole deal.

Enough of this. Back to getting breakfast. My turn back to the wheezing Roy has shown that it is indeed a rather large glass or red, nary a sign of cork in it. Perfect. A steady lean down to the table and-

The other knee!-

Cracking in sympathy with the other, it seems. Trying to get between me and my breakfast juice, eh? Wait. No, no reaction from himself. And it's in my hand, warm and safe, light pouring beautifully through the window and the glass. To greet the day. Defoe, was it who wrote that? Some dead bastard. Why am I asking, I don't care. It's what I'm doing, the best way of doing it.

A nice warm wake-up of a drink, is what it is. Of course, now I'm awake and drinking I might need to go for a piss at some point, but – no. Think about that crisis when it comes. Enjoy this, for now. Second glug. Someone else's drink, of course. Always tastes better. And how is that certain someone? Still slumped. Snoring abated. Oh wait. Bad sign, that might mean that he's about to wake up. You're a nice old friend, Roy, but far better to know when you're asleep and I'm pinching your wine. And you do have a tendency to start crying when you wake up hungover and dishevelled, I've found out that much over the years. Not something I can be bollocksed do deal with at present.

He's twitching. So an awakening may be coming to pass. Skedaddle and leave him to it. Can't do the stairs, between the floor's creaking and my knees I'll have the whole street up, let alone himself. Ah yes, of course, front room. I know this place like the back of my face, even if I can't remember how to get to it. Sun coming in through the front windows, bit of billowing curtain, this will make a nice morning's awning, potentially. As long as I'm left alone. Quality of light, christ I could get poetic here – time for another sip – yes, it's a gentle buttery hue of indirect sunlight god how different to the retina melting blast you get from set lights, far better, although-

-oh god, the film. The bloody film, how did we get from there to here? Smoke, smoke and the angry mermen, no. No. Don't think about it. Trouble was happening alright and all you did was successfully extricate yourself from it. They'll be glad to see you well. Thing was almost done, as I recall. And can't be done without you. Phew. Yes. And as for the trouble? Eh, now wherever it roared up from you can't have been the cause. No, just some local characters taking against you. It happened before, didn't it? When that crew had to be flown out of Caracas especially. I could not be blamed then, they were an aggressive lot whoever they were. Stupid idea to leave the city and shoot in the jungle. But what harm came of it in the end, we just shot the rest of it on a soundstage in Hertfordshire, and did it look any bad?

Well, I have no idea, do I? Fucked if I could be bothered to see it. Come to think of it, why wasn't this shot indoors, somewhere. What daft fucker in Illinois or Mumbai will want to spend a couple of hours of their life looking at some fuzzy scrag of an English seaside town that even the English don't want to visit? And more to the point, with me all over it?

Of course, the patron wanted it, the unseen funder. Wanted you, that is. Why is not to question. It was money to be taken, even if it felt like some mad imagining. Well, maybe it's all been the spasming of a dying mind, all this. Yes, I saw that obituary, my obituary, unmistakably flapping out onto an underground line. But no. Reject that, surely that's too trite a trope? You're alive. Yes, and mildly disappointed to be so. And if all the last six week's happenings do turn out to be only your collapsing mind, call it Incident at Owl Creek. Heh!

Now. Some movement in that chair. High backed green chair, yes someone is there. Covered in some old coats. I must have laughed out loud. How long that thought tentacle reached out for, I don't know but I've been stood here with the wine, swaying in the sun and do doubt creaking. More movement. Please stay asleep, do you know how much interaction I've had to pretend to endure recently?

I see a young hand. Female.

Oh god, the girl from the shoot. Laura. How did she get here. Why did she get here? Did? No. That's decades out of the question. Did I try- no. No, I remember nothing but yapping with Roy. I don't even think of that kind of thing now, can't remember the last time I did. Or thought about making it happen. And especially with someone who is so young they look like they don't know what life is.

Why? There was some connection, some job. Of course, yes. She was the one sent to make sure I wasn't taking the air every night. Obvious dogsbody, or someone desperate to impress the fat rich boy director, and producer, and camera fecker. Yes. Sent to look after me like a childminder. Me, minded by a child.

I should at the very least be reflecting on the resting inexplicable beauty of youth or something, but I'm just being made to feel very old and annoyed that somehow this near foetal character is in my territory and impinging in my light. Literally. Now, that's the sign of being a poet rather than an actor.

Still no sign of her waking, thank god. I had no desire to talk to any of that brigade of babbies more than was contractually necessary to do so. I don't want to start now when instead there's a good chance I could actually be enjoying myself.

Now look, you old weirdo, look to what it's come to. Decades of afterparties, wrap parties and post party parties and did you ever think that you'd actively want to kick a young one out of the room? No. No, the beast that I was ran on it. Lived on it. But at some point the young ones did nothing but get younger whilst suddenly you were older than all and sundry, and those poles flew apart. You old letch, what happened to that old beast? What happened is, I withdrew, somehow. Yes, but only after all recoiled from you. And why? Was it just age, eh, just beginning to show, well what was it then, middle age finally creeping in? Did the shame come from inside outward, or slowly close in upon you? Making you finally wither down to what you are now, a sad old man recoiling from someone in case they wake and see you, you with your morning wine?

Look at the young. What world do we have together? I'm saying goodbye to everyone alive but especially the young. No, I'm not saying goodbye to them, I'm getting rid of them. Look at her, there. Bet she's never gone hungry in her life, never endured a real hardship. Not slightly, otherwise why would she have found herself working on a pointless film set?

To think that when it all stopped, that was so long ago. Decades. After a good couple of decades of not having any end to it in sight, all that. No woman resisted me. No woman said no. As far as I can recall. I had second hand notoriety, it provided the introduction before I'd ever walked into any room. I must, must have spent time in active pursuit of it all but for all the time I have left, I can't remember ever doing so. The work just happened to me, and so did the women. With all those poor saps left out in the cold, looking in, the ones who were trying, trying to get to where I was and not understanding at all: this either happens to you or it doesn't. Everything happened to me.

Yeah, all the women who wanted me, until they had me. Then it was too late. Perhaps that what caused it to all fall away; word finally got out that whether it became apparent after a few days or a few children this man wasn't worth the hazard. And when word did finally get out it stayed there and you were left to crumble into this state. No. No, lying to yourself again, you know it. If you have a modicum of fame and notoriety and it's obvious that you're more trouble than its worth, that won't stop the women lining up. Not by a long chalk. The recoiling came from within. And for that judgement of not being worth the bother, you know very well that you're trying to black out the worst of it. Always whirling at the edge of your mind. The quadruple betrayals, the flying fists, all the regular stuff they all suffered.

True, it is true and I've never denied that, not to myself. I'd rather not dwell. Many of these matters were common things to experience in a marriage in those times. A raised fist was merely a more underlined slap, and they were common enough to see in others' differences. I am a product of my time, which is nearly done. Part of this is that I will keep any shame to myself. As if anyone else would be interested, mind, but no. Within this skull the thoughts will stay. Not worth sharing even with those who are still alive, from what I can remember, and occasionally form into perfect view in my mind's eye. More sleepless nights as they stare me down, every time. No. It is not in my psyche to blather out about any of this, and what good would it do? Um? My question to all those I see mimsying about on the chat shows nowdays, sharing their tales of abuse received or given, what are they doing it for? Understanding or exoneration? Or ascension of the career ladder? Don't make me any more sick than I undoubtedly am. I will stick to my mode, shame and regrets are to be kept within myself.

Well there I go, got carried away with myself again. How long did that crash of though last? It appears she's still asleep. Good. And I can hear Roy snoring again in the back room. Still some time for peace, then.

I stayed awake through the whole thing. I'd woken up when I heard some creaky commotion in the room behind me, but didn't want to move. Way too unsure of where I was or how I'd got there. And when the memories blasted back into me, I didn't move out of sheer fear. So yeah, that's the final image I have of Dermot, kind of how I'll always remember him. And unfortunately I think I'll always remember him. Stood swaying in the doorway, definitely looking my way. Glass of red already still in his hand, like a wheezing spectre. You know those creaks, those little snappings that old people make even when they're not moving much? That was the only sound in the room then, apart from my suppressed breathing. Boy was I grateful for whatever heavy coat I'd thrown over myself for warmth. I don't think he realised I was awake and could see, I really don't. But of all the times I was frightened over those bloody weird weeks, that was the last and the quietest.

What he was thinking, I don't know. I've always thought that he'd been in plenty of similar situations over the years, with equally unguarded young women. Just my hunch. And I wonder what happened to them. And I wonder what made him turn away then.

I stayed still until I heard the slow, deliberate footsteps disappear outside. It wasn't just me he was trying to keep from waking. When I could be sure, I slid the coat down. The room I was in was some kind of old world wooden drawing room, it would have looked genteel and respectable if anyone had given it any respect over the years. Between the khol and gunk in my eyes I made out a couple of dusty stuffed parrots, newspapers lobbed over every chair and corner, mirrors that were so epically stained they were giving off virtually no reflection.

The continued shock hit me in another low wave. The day before I'd been still slugging it out on that set, now I was- where? Where was this, had the tweedy man driven us back to London or were we in some other little stinker of a forgotten town? Or worse, were we still near enough to the set that I could be found? I slid a clammy hand into my right jeans pocket. The phone was still there, not mine, the work phone that meant I could be contacted by Hero or David or some other associated minion. I held it and rubbed the greasy screen. It was still off. Off, perhaps totally dead, which would be even better. For the first time since waking up, I was conscious of exhaling. It would stay off. I'd decided that much.

Some shuffling noise came through from another room, definitely not Dermot noises. Unless there was a wife or other partner there (and looking at the evidence, I thought it wildly unlikely) it had to be the tweedy bloke. A groan topped off the shuffling and it sounded like the voice I remembered making out above the sound of the car and the road. In comparison to Dermot he had seemed like a normal enough human being, no – he'd seemed like a human being. Still, I wasn't sure about him, purely by association. The voice whispered around the door –

-You awake in there?

-If I say yes, I must be.

-Come on in, if you want.

I looked around on another room of knackered armchairs and decaying things. He was still in his tweeds, and fixing up some concoction at a table. I guessed that the nearest he'd got to bed was the flattened sofa next to him.

-Drink?

-Do you have coffee?

-Yes, but that's not for today.

-Right, what's that then?

-Gin. With orange. Morning concession.

-No thanks. Can I just have some orange?

-Sorry m'dear, that's only for the gin.

He looked even odder whilst upright. The tiny glasses had bent themselves during whatever sleep he'd managed to get, but the rest of his face had seemed to have folded itself over on the sofa as well. Half or it was reddened with an imprint of the distressed leather. Still, despite looking on the wrong side of eccentric I wasn't getting any creepy vibes off him. Actually, more the opposite – I was an amusing afterthought.

-You'll have some explaining to do. Dermot was saying you're part of the crew. I thought you were just another hotel guest caught up in the commotion.

-I am. Was. Both. Look, where are we?

-Well, we 'aint near there, if you're trying to make it back.

-I'm not. I'm done with it.

-I'm guessing they won't be happy with you absconding. Jumping before you have to walk the plank?

-If you put it like that, yeah, yeah. You know he's supposed to be the lead in the bloody thing?

-He'd mentioned it. I was as perplexed as he was.

-He's still needed. And I was supposed to be keeping him out of trouble.

In response to this he wheezed and wobbled. His face grew worryingly pink.

-Well it's nice that you all tried...

He drank from his morning mix.

-...but last night's kind of stuff always happened. Well, not for a while. But then again, he hadn't been employed in a while. Bloody fools, all of you.

There was no malice in that, more amusement. Thankfully his pinkness had receded. I could see that he was old enough-early sixties, perhaps? But one of those older blokes who looked as if they'd still go stealing apples from gardens, or whatever they did back then.

-You've known him for a while?

-I've tolerated him for decades. And he gives me a call once in a while. Of course, I'm happy to answer when it comes through. More surprised that he's alive and can make his way around a telephone, than anything else.

So Dermot actually had someone to almost call a friend. Improbable.

-I'm guessing he was nicer in his younger days, then?

He paused.

-Not really. But he was more successful. Nights out with him were a guaranteed event. The stories I could tell you...

Don't, I thought. Please don't.

-...I sometimes wonder if they're true myself. You know O'Toole locked us in the Old Vic overnight, once? For some prank. The management found us and weren't happy at all.

-O'Toole?

-The very same, Peter.

-No idea. Another friend of yours, I'm guessing.

For the first time, his face fell. The glass was empty, but he slowly started to change that.

-Look, I'm not going back to that set, if Dermot wants to he'll be doing it himself. I need to know how to get back to...

Back to what, I wondered. What and where? Another wave of shock hit me in the calves. Back to the rented room I barely knew, people I hadn't seen for – how long? I knew everything was over. Everything I'd been trying and striving and sacrificing and working twenty hour days would be utterly negated by my latest actions. I'd abandoned set and allowed the lead to disappear, during a fracas that the police were surely picking over right now. Whatever mad luck that set had been running on had surely vanished now. And I'd abandoned set. No doubt if I switched the phone on I'd have reams of voicemails and messages from the crew, saying – well, I could guess.

I couldn't stay in this place. But where could I go to? I had my wallet and there was enough of the measly per diems to get me somewhere, I knew that. And that was the rotten piece of driftwood that my mind clung to.

-If it's London you're after, there's train connections. Not that far, we're well inland. He's pulled this kind of stunt before, you know. I'm amazed that people have continued to employ him after the time he's done it. When they knew he'd almost certainly do it – kind of like a woman going back to a husband who...eh...

-I get the picture.

-But I think he's really fucked it now. Even if he had more time left, I've never seen a palaver like that at the hotel yesterday.

-I'm glad to hear that. Really am.

-Yes, I mean lunatics like him always attract their own kind. But that was genuinely crazed. Better than any theatre I've seen in the last few years.

-And we left at the interval.

A yelp.

-Yes! All that and we pissed off to get pissed. I'll nick that if you don't mind, m'dear. You're not bad, you've got a wit about you.

He looked down at the glass which was empty again.

-Mean you're fucked on that front as well, I'm afraid.

-I know. That's fine, I'm sick of it. I think I'd better try something new. Whatever I can.

-You're a young pup.

-I'm twenty seven, thanks.

-Like I said, a young pup.

-Right. It was my ambition in life, since I was a teenager.

-Not a long chunk of your life, then, although I appreciate that it is from your perspective. Look, you can either make a success of it, or get booted out and do something different. Sometimes I think the luckier ones end up with the latter. I mean, look at...

He gestured somewhere out back to where Dermot was presumably lurking.

-Catastrophic success. He got what everyone else wanted. And you have the look of someone who's been striving. All the time.

-For diminishing returns.

-And tell me this - for the few better times, the bits of supposed success, how did they feel?

-I'll only admit now that it doesn't feel as if they were worth it.

-Don't waste it. It's vanishing.

I knew what he was referring to. I'd had to hesitate when giving my age. Twenty two, three, four? No-

-But hey, stick with it and you may end up as happy and well adjusted as us two reprobates. No, best to be like Roberto Duran.

-Another friend of yours, right?

-No, no. Boxer. Big boxer, until he decided he'd had enough, wasn't going to let it all end with some younger git splattering his face all over the canvas. Realised a fight wasn't going his way and just raised his fists in the air, crying out No Mas! No mas! That's it, no more. When you've had enough, quit how you want to. Don't let some herbert have one over you.

-Nice. Did he have anything to do with the band?

-Right, now it's my turn to not get it.

-Duran – there was a band called that wasn't there?

-Duran Duran? Yes, he set it up with his brother. Who was a mime.

-Really?

-It's a lovely image.

-I really must leave.

Although, I must say that I didn't mind the company. Odd as he was, this old barker was the only person I'd really spoken to outside of the crew in over a month. Maybe because of this, he wasn't trying to get me to do something for him. No, I had to leave because I wanted my life to be ever further away from that set than it already was. I also had a creeping realisation that unless he'd was passed out or actually died, Dermot would be making a return soon.

-Well, I can give you directions, or a lift..

-You won't give me a lift.

-Fair enough, m'dear. Before you go, I thought this might amuse you. You know, he's been half sure that he's actually dead these last few weeks?

-Dead? Well, he's always looked haunted.

-Considering half of the things he's gotten up to, that's how it should be. No, I mean he's convinced that he saw his own obituary in a paper on the tube.

-Fuck! Now that would freak me out-

-Well, it's a nice image, isn't it? Thing is, I know the truth. Some poor sap of an economics professor carked it recently. Same name, Dermot Boyle. Seems some wally in one of the less-read papers pulled that old sod's obit out instead, it ran before they could pull it. I'm trying to get a back issue so I can wave it in his face. Maybe that would get rid of him for good, eh? And there's a way to go!

He was wheezing his way into pinkness again. And I'll admit, I was laughing.

-I tried to tell him the truth last night, but oh, he's a broken record. Well, he'll find out. And they'll be right one day.

-He'll never get to read the full thing.

-Brutal truth is, I'm surprised that at least one of the papers has an obituary of him to hand. He isn't generally remembered. And when he is, it tends not to be with fondness

-Look, er..

-Roy. S'Roy. And you're..?

-Laura.

-Right. Apologies for my tardiness in not remembering earlier.'

-I wouldn't worry. If he's such a monster, why stick around with him?

-Few do, but few do with me, either. I guess, Laura, that's one of the mysteries of friendship.

A long, almost subsonic groan came from the garden. Dermot was waking.

Roy looked up from his glass.

-Elude him.

London

2007.

I've enjoyed recollecting all this with you. It's nice to realise how far away I've gotten from all of that madness. I'd been leaving it all festering in the back of my head, but talking about it all crystallises the memories, puts them into relief. I can see how different things are.

Yes, so I fled. Happily. I felt that I was on the run for a while, really thought I'd have a lawsuit or some other showdown on my hands. The mobile phone went straight in the Thames as soon as I'd staggered out of Charing Cross. After a few weeks, no angry emails from the production company came through. I wasn't pursuing them in any way. Oh yeah the per diems stopped instantly but hey, I had no objection to that. Keep your dogsbody money. After jittery few weeks I realised that they weren't bothering. I'd been saved by my own insignificance.

And that sad old ghoul is dead. No big obituary that I saw, just a small couple of paragraphs that I caught whist skimming the Standard on a lunch break. He was found slumped in the Pavilion Gardens in Brighton, comatose after what must have been, even by his standards, a particularly feral binge. Couldn't be revived. The little article summarised his career by calling him a star of several cult horror films from the sixties. I never knew, and I'm afraid to say that I can't remember anyone from the crew saying anything about that. Starr of cult horror films? He was a horror, and a complete cult.

What? Oh look, I know you're not supposed to speak ill of the dead, but given all the grief he created...I do keep thinking about what old Roy said though. If Dermot wasn't quite sure if he was alive or dead, what was that final Brighton binge about? Was he trying to put something to the test? From what I can glean about his life he'd already lived it as if there were no consequences. Well for him it seems there rarely was, the consequences seem to have been suffered by the unfortunates in his orbit. Especially now, I recoil from that kind of life. The sense of shapelessness, neverending self indulgence. I wonder, once you've been like that for a while, is it even possible to get out of the quicksand and re-order things? Well, you'd have to want to, obviously. Never got any sense of that from him, not that I can say that we were ever on intimate terms. Thank god.

I suppose if you were listening to someone else's story, you could have expected some kind of connection, rapproachment or revelation between him and I. Come off it, my old shadow. Life 'aint like that, so neither is my story. No neat pat ending, that would be like something straight from the film.

So yes I've smarted up, got a job, I could almost say settled down...well, the years of instability kind of precluded any ability to have any of the main markers of a normal life, like routines, relationships, a healthy sense of self. Yes, I'm now the kind of person who'll happily drop the word precluded into a sentence, I've come along in the world. Far, far away from that downward treadmill. I can't tell you what I do for a living. I mean, I know what it is, but when I tell people they tend to glaze over. Ok, I mostly stare at spreadsheets – anxiously. Sounds shit but I don't mind it and it pays the bills. Kind of the opposite to when I'd tell people that I worked in film and it'd sound great but the reality was shit.

Oh yes, and the film itself. Defying everyone's expectations it was actually finished, shoot completed somehow, edited into some form of narrative and released into the world with such a paltry promotional budget that I'd be surprised if anyone more than the production company saw it. On for a couple of weeks on one of the dinkier screens in the Soho Curzon. Did I watch it? Did I hell. Come on, I may have nearly broken my sanity for it but for all my work, nothing I did would have been up on screen, would it? Oh, and they settled on a title. Autumn Reunion. Yes really, they settled for that. I mean that tells you all you need to know, doesn't it? They couldn't even be arsed to come up with something that gave off a modicum of fizz or intrigue. Something tells me that all concerned found that they'd created a lumpen stinker and they gave it the blandest came they could in order to cloak it. Hidden. Perhaps.

Well, I know one person who saw it. My housemate insisted on doing so, although that may be partly because she's one of the few people I know who watches pretty much everything that comes out. Now, she's not one for vague opinions, but between the credits rolling and her getting home, the thing seemed to vanish from her memory. Sunday night telly, that was the most she could say. Ah yes, and the fact that they got around Dermot's premature exit by shooting around it, apparently the story (and camera) focused on the lead actress a lot more. I'm sure she didn't object. Can you blame them?

Oh, and Hero, the producer, turned up as a talking head on some vapid arts show I caught by accident recently. Not talking about the film of course (who'd want to ask him?), no he was blathering on about one of his film icons, some Italian bloodbath merchant. They showed a couple of clips of the subject's stuff, it made me feel ill. Usual women-butchering. Yeah carry on with your self-promotion you great bellowing man child. I have a feeling everything will work out for you just fine. I looked him up online afterward, I love how all the info on these bods is there to find now, easily. Turns out he was even posher than I'd guessed, but more interestingly there was a reason for the name. I'm not sure whether the shortening is better, but I can see the reasoning. His parents hadn't lumbered him with the name of Hero at first, they'd given him the full horror of Hieronymus. I dread to think what kind of people they are, and have a new found understanding of his desire to order the world in his own way.

So there you go, hundreds of people are lashed together to make a piece of work, they all go mad and some get paid; then it disappears into the ether. Maybe these things aren't supposed to make sense, maybe it's like that in other places and other endeavours. I know that right now, so many people are trying to break into it, not realising that they're hurling themselves like lemmings. Or lemons.

I was one. And perhaps it's worth spending the prime of your youth almost drowning in that lunatic river, I'm not so sure. The films from university, they're still saved away safely, but I know I won't watch them. And I have no desire for anyone else to see them; and after all isn't that the key to it all?

For now I'm glad that I've found the strength to stop pursuing an ambition that may have been smoke and mirrors. I've quit chasing after a version of what life could be, it's time to stand still and let life happen. Let life tell you who you are rather than try to impose it yourself, after all you may be the one who knows the least anyway.

So thanks for this, it's been a dispatch from a weird time in my life. I'm glad to say I'm now at the stage where I can bid it all a smiling goodbye. Smiling but yes, a definite goodbye.

Printed in Great Britain
by Amazon